# FORSAKEN FALLOUT

## Haunted Wastelands Series

## BOOK 3

# IAN FORTEY
### AND
# RON RIPLEY

EDITED BY ANNE LAO
AND DAWN KLEMISH

ISBN: 979-8-89476-292-0
Copyright © 2025 by ScareStreet.com

*This is a work of fiction. Any resemblance to actual persons, living or dead, or actual events is purely coincidental.*

## Enter the Realm of Terror…

We'd like to take a moment to thank you for your support and invite you to join our VIP newsletter.

Dive deeper into the darkness with exclusive offers, early access to new releases, and bone-chilling deals when you sign up at www.ScareStreet.com.

Let the nightmares begin…

See you in the shadows,
Scare Street

# PROLOGUE

The skies had opened. Desert lightning isn't like lightning everywhere else. The openness made it seem so much bigger and more intense. The smell of desert-meets-storm was an experience. Two opposing forces coming together with no care for what got caught in the middle.

Dezzy trudged across the wet sand. Rain pelted his face and soaked his clothes. He wore shorts and a T-shirt, an old pair of sneakers, and nothing more except for a backpack slung over one shoulder that steadily grew heavier in the rain. He had not expected to fight the elements. His long, dark hair was plastered to his face, and every so often, a gust of wind sent a chill up his back.

The man at his side was untouched by the weather. He had his own problems. Doc's flesh was partially melted into an ever-dripping ooze that hung from his face, hands, and every inch of his body like it might all slough away at any moment. Some of it did. It dripped into the sand with the rainwater but quickly faded away. No part of him could exist separated from the whole.

Doc's skull, the item that bound his spirit to the world, was in Dezzy's backpack. Doc did not like being out in the open because he feared that the radiation saturating his bones would harm the living. Dezzy had assured him it might be a problem for others, but he would be fine. Dezzy was dead for decades once. He was not built like other people.

Dezzy did not think that Doc was dangerous. He didn't have any tools to measure radiation, but he suspected Doc was being a little paranoid. Or perhaps it wasn't so much that he would hurt people as it was that he was ashamed to face them.

Dezzy hadn't pried too deeply into what Doc had done at the lab. He knew enough to know that he was responsible for hurting people. He believed that Doc was punishing himself for what he had done. Punishing himself even beyond death. He felt like he deserved to be locked away for eternity for his crimes.

It wasn't Dezzy's place to tell anyone what sort of penance they did or didn't deserve. That was a very personal thing. In Dezzy's opinion, Doc had suffered enough.

There were no lights in the desert, nor were there signposts or even roads. Dezzy was following his gut. Something had come up from under the sand and devoured the town of Benton right in front of him. Something that was not alive. And it had disappeared into the restricted areas of the Nevada desert. The place where Thomas Coulson had gone with Shane Ryan and the FBI agent whose name he forgot. Venti? Venison? It didn't matter.

If anyone could stop what he had seen, it was Thomas Coulson. And if Coulson had elected to go to Shane Ryan and the FBI agent for help, then he'd need them, too. But he had to find them first, and they had gone in search of Doc's old lab.

Getting through the desert had, up to that point, not been difficult. They came across an abandoned guard post at a fence. Dezzy simply opened the gate and let himself in. The most difficult part of the journey was the distance. He didn't have a car, so he was on foot. When a torrential downpour began, that slowed him more.

Dezzy grew up in Arizona and had experienced desert life in the past. The Sonoran Desert was not the Mojave, but storms like the one he and Doc were experiencing had to be just as rare there as they were back home. He took it as a sign that something needed to be done quickly.

Walking was not the hardship for Dezzy so much as the time lost to it. His goal was so far away, and the desert was so vast. Coulson was not a man who waited around. He was a mover, and he couldn't sit still. All

Dezzy could do was follow his instincts and some basic directions from Doc.

The storm raged on. Flashes of lightning illuminated figures in the dark. Sometimes, Dezzy saw a ghost roaming the desert alone. When they neared the rocky hills, he saw many more. They watched him pass, as still and silent as statues. A palpable fear was in the air that the rain could not drown out. He had seen things that scared the dead before, and none of them were good.

It took hours before they reached a second fence, though this one was in shambles and not as large as the unguarded entry fence. Instead, it was set up as a perimeter around a small structure. Much of the fence had been knocked down, but a few posts remained upright and supported broken panels of chain link and razor wire.

"This is it, this is the lab," Doc said as they approached. "Something has happened, though."

Doc's eyes were better in the dark than Dezzy's, but it didn't take a ghost to realize a massive hole was in the ground next to the fence line. The thing he had seen in Benton had also visited this place.

The structure was concrete, a slanted roof like a small shed that concealed a set of giant steel doors that had somehow been melted. The steel was resting in blobs in the doorframe much like the flesh eternally drooling off Doc's face.

Dezzy approached the lab entrance carefully. Doc had worked there many years ago, doing experiments he no longer liked to talk about because of the shame he felt. He died doing the work, and so did a lot of other people. Dezzy didn't hold it against him. He had met his share of saints and sinners, and, in the end, they all ended up in the ground.

Rainwater ran freely into the open door, and Dezzy heard it falling and splattering far below. Doc led him to the stairs that descended into the depths of the lab. With no light, there was not a lot to see, and Dezzy's eyes were now almost useless.

They reached the first floor, and some red emergency lighting in the hall illuminated a destroyed door and a burned hallway beyond. Dezzy peered inside, watching a pair of ghosts who seemed oblivious to his presence sway gently.

"These were our failures," Doc said. "They are less than they were. Conscious but not really thinking."

"Who were they?" Dezzy asked.

Doc looked at him, and then back at the ghosts in the burned-out hallway.

"I never knew. I never asked. If they had names, families, or histories, knowing would have been too much on my conscience."

"But you said they volunteered," Dezzy whispered.

Doc nodded.

"Yes. But no one volunteered to become what these things are."

"Why did you keep doing the experiments?"

"Because," Doc said, "to quit would mean this was for nothing. In my mind, it was worse to not continue. If you wage war, you must kill men. And they say it is for the greater good. But if you lose that war, then did you not kill all those men for nothing? Is your loss not so much greater now? I wanted to succeed to make it mean something. To make it just."

They stood in silence, shoulder to shoulder, watching the swaying ghosts. Their burned bodies looked like nightmares come to life. The whole lab looked like something from a horrible accident.

In his first life, Dezzy had not thought much about the balance of life and death, or if some deaths were just and others were not. That changed after he died. He had met many souls in his time, those who had passed beyond the mortal world and had become something more and something less at the same time.

Not everyone who died deserved it; he knew that now. And sometimes, people who died deserved a much worse fate than they got. But death was all that life had to offer at the end of things. Just or not, it was meted out equally to everyone.

"Was it just?" Dezzy asked.

"No, Dezzy," Doc answered. "There was nothing just about any of my work. I was a foolish, ignorant man. That is my legacy."

Doc was not alone in that feeling. If there was one thing death was good at, it was making a person appreciate what they had done wrong in life. Death gave life to regret. Unfortunately, most people just had to deal with that for the rest of eternity. Most people didn't get a chance to return to fix things.

Dezzy tried not to focus on Doc and his turmoil over things done and not. He needed to focus on the present. He needed to help his friend.

There was no sign that Coulson had been in the burned lab, so Dezzy turned his back on it and headed down the stairs to the next level. It was gutted like the first. There were no ghosts there, just destruction. They gave the floor a cursory look, but there was nothing to see. The water continued to splatter on the floor below them, and Dezzy followed it down.

It was not until they reached the very bottom of the lab that Dezzy discovered some indication of what had happened recently. Water pooled there, a couple of inches deep before it ran over the doorframe and into the final lab space, where it quickly ran into an enormous hole in the floor. The thing from Benton had been here as well.

Dezzy walked carefully around the hole, avoiding where the water had made it slick. It looked like more of the broken floor could have caved into the chasm, and he didn't want to fall in. Instead, he made his way to the far side of the lab space, illuminated by red emergency lights stuck to the walls near the ceiling. A computer was there, a control panel of some kind.

"I knew I should have taken a computer course, man," Dezzy muttered. He had spent most of the rise of the digital age dead and far from technology. His experience with computers was very limited, but he was open to giving it a whirl if Doc would guide him through it.

"This was not my lab," Doc said, "but I can help you."

"This wasn't your place? I thought that was where we were going," Dezzy said.

"No. I worked on Phase Two. That doesn't matter now. I think this was the Phase Three lab. Press that button there to turn the computer on."

Dezzy did as instructed, and nothing happened. The computer screens remained blank. Nothing lit up or whirred or did whatever computers were meant to do. He pressed the button again with a frown, hoping maybe if he did it harder, he would kick something in gear.

"Perhaps it was damaged by… whatever happened." Doc gestured to the hole in the floor.

Dezzy grunted. He knew they were supposed to go to the lab. Or he knew it as well as he knew anything in life. His feelings were generally right about things like that. Maybe a holdover from returning from the dead, but he had reliable instincts. He always ended up where he needed to be. At least, he thought he did.

He tried more buttons, but the computer was a lost cause. There was no hope of learning anything from it. Maybe his instincts were not working as well as he had hoped. He hadn't foreseen what happened in the town of Benton. Maybe he was not up to the task anymore, or maybe something was affecting his intuition.

Dezzy turned away and paused. On the wall, under one of the red emergency lights, was a map. It showed where they were, a series of bunkers, and three additional labs.

"What's this?" Dezzy pointed to the map.

The ghost looked over his shoulder at a fifth location on the map, adjacent to the lab they were in. The borders were drawn with a dotted line.

"That was the Project Five facility. It is entirely subterranean," Doc answered.

"What's Project Five?"

"I don't know," Doc admitted. "I learned soon enough that asking questions got one nowhere. I did my work, and that was all."

Dezzy looked at the map again, and then at the wall near the hole in the floor. Someone had tunneled through there as well. This was smaller and more like something made by a man. And it was in the direction of the Project Five facility.

"So, do you think we'd end up here," Dezzy pointed to where Project Five was on the map, "if we went through that hole in the wall?"

"I don't know," Doc answered.

"Guess we'll find out, man."

With Doc at his heels, Dezzy darted around the destroyed floor and entered the smaller tunnel. He was quickly consumed by darkness, leaving the red emergency lights behind and fumbling along a grossly uneven path.

Dezzy didn't feel fear as he traveled into the dark tunnel. He remembered fear, and he supposed he still had a sense of it, but it wasn't the way it used to be. Even when he found himself in life-threatening situations, fear wasn't the same as it had been before he died the first time.

Doc guided him as best as he could, but uneven footing made Dezzy stumble several times. It took several minutes of tripping and stubbing his toes on rocky protrusions before the tunnel opened into a larger cavern.

A faint glow came from the center of the chamber. The cave looked natural, something the tunnel had broken into, but the glow was not. It came from a room and a metal box built inside the cave a short distance from the tunnel.

Great, jagged teeth of stone rose from the ground in the cavern, and Dezzy couldn't remember if they were stalagmites or stalactites. Either way, they reached his waist and looked like the open jaws of a stony beast that had fallen asleep with a steel box in its mouth.

He and Doc approached the metal structure and the glow that came from within it. It reminded Dezzy of a bank vault, only something had torn it to pieces. The door and part of the front wall had been ripped apart. The marks in the metal looked like claws, and he did not have to think hard to imagine what had done it.

The cavern around the vault looked like Swiss cheese, a patchwork of tunnels at all angles. Some were as small as the one Dezzy had used to enter the chamber, but others were much larger, easily ten feet across.

"It's lead." Doc drew Dezzy's attention back to the vault.

Dezzy touched the metal and nodded. The interior was all lead. No ghost should have been able to escape from it, but it had been destroyed from the inside out.

Beyond the door, in what remained of the vault, was a mass grave. Bodies lay upon bodies. Some were ancient, burned skeletons but others were fresh. Others were ones he recognized, like the waitress from the Fission Chips diner. The people of Benton were piled there, dozens of bodies, broken and battered. Many were unrecognizable, and some were barely identifiable as human.

In the center of the vault was a twisted form of merged bodies, bones fused onto bones like a tangle of weeds that glowed with an eerie, blue-green light. Dezzy had never seen anything like it in life or in death. Countless bodies were warped into a single skeleton, a structure for some unthinkable nightmare.

"What is that?" he asked quietly.

"I don't know," Doc answered. "I don't want to find out."

Some of the bodies still bore clothing on their dehydrated and burned frames. Dezzy saw lab coats, scorched and half-melted, merging with military uniforms, jumpsuits, and even a suit and tie.

Even though he did not know what it was, Dezzy knew what he was seeing. It was the body of the thing that had attacked Benton. The thing that had swallowed the town and brought the dead back to the vault. Back to its nest.

What Dezzy didn't know was why a ghost—or whatever the thing he had seen was—wanted more bodies.

"We need to go," he said. "We need to find Coulson and Shane Ryan. Now."

He ran from the vault, and Doc did not protest. The desert was vast, but there was a map on the wall. There were only so many places to look.

He just hoped he had the time.

# Chapter 1
# Behind Enemy Lines

Shane sat still in the back of the Humvee, listening to the patter of rain and paying attention to the motion of the vehicle as well as he could. They had traveled straight for quite a while before taking a sharp left turn and descending. Some of the motion had been too hard to discern. Did they take a soft curve or continue straight?

With a black bag over his head, he could not see where they were going, and none of the men in the vehicle were speaking, so he was doing his best to track their progress and make a map in his head. They had gone farther east than he had traveled with Ventura or Coulson before, but as far as he knew, that was taking them well off grid for any of the maps he had previously looked at. They were in uncharted territory.

The men who had taken him and Ventura—Hawke and his soldiers—bore no recognizable military rank or insignia. They could have been Army, Air Force, or nothing official. They had the gear, and they were in the right place, but there was no way to know who they were for real. He suspected they would not be forthcoming if he asked.

Ventura had been taken with him, though neither had spoken since they were forced into the Humvee. Coulson was missing. He had done something to destroy the Burnt Souls and then returned to assist with Sergeant Dylan, but he had not appeared since.

Shane knew Coulson was not gone. Whatever had happened to him hadn't destroyed him, but fighting the Burners and Burnt Souls had taken its toll. Shane just hoped he was able to pull himself together. Coulson was smart. If he thought it was too risky to interfere, he would have held back.

It was too early to make many guesses about what was happening.

Coulson was not like other ghosts, so there was no way to predict where he was or what was going on. For all Shane knew, he could have been trailing them. Because Shane had a bag on his head, Coulson could have been in the Humvee, and Shane still wouldn't have known.

The man called Hawke had been dispassionate about his work. He was neither angry nor amused when he arrived to take them into custody. He was indifferent. Businesslike. But he knew both of their names without asking, and Shane did not like that. It meant someone had been watching them for a while. Someone knew they were in the desert and had waited to come for them.

Sgt. Dylan, the Phase Three experiment, was gone. But the Waste was not. Whatever Hawke was doing, it would only cost him and many others in the long run. They needed something powerful to take out the ghost known as the Waste, something much more powerful than even Shane and Coulson together.

The Waste was a conglomeration of death, a fused body of perhaps dozens of corpses that the PULSE experiments in the desert had created by accident. While they were busy making ghosts that could wield and control the power of a nuclear weapon, they had inadvertently created a thing that became one ghost made of many when the dead bodies that created it fused in a devastating accident. Now, it seemed devoid of reason or even human thought. It was like a beast that tunneled below the earth. Even iron and lead could not keep it at bay or contain it. And it was feasting on the dead.

Shane was not afraid to take on a challenge. He had fought against the odds many times in the past. But the Waste was something different. He had fought a tiny version of it, a piece that must have fallen off the whole, and it was a struggle. Each piece that was destroyed meant nothing to the larger nightmare. It could continue to exist, move, and fight. It would be like destroying dozens of spirits at the same time with no waiting. To confront the entire beast would be certain death.

The Humvee came to a stop and rain pelted the roof like the marching of a thousand boots. Doors opened and still no one spoke. A hand grabbed Shane by the arm and pulled him roughly out of the vehicle. He stumbled, almost losing his footing on the wet earth.

"Where are we?" he heard Ventura ask. No one answered him.

There was more sound. Something hollow, and multiple footsteps. Several doors closed. The pauses were just as important as the moments when things were happening. Something was being communicated to those around him who could see. Silent orders, he assumed.

The hand on Shane's arm tugged him forward, and he started marching through the rain. His captors were not needlessly aggressive. Everything was businesslike and efficient. Whoever Hawke was, he wasn't blowing smoke or intimidating. He was beyond that.

"Can you take this off?" Ventura said.

The bag was saturated with rainwater on Shane's head, and the fabric clung to his face. If he didn't hang his head at the right angle, it sucked against his nose and mouth as he breathed, and it felt like he was drowning. The effect was not unlike being waterboarded.

He heard a dull thud and a grunt from Ventura. Someone hit him, maybe in the gut or maybe in the face, but he did not speak again. So they weren't beyond using force if they felt it necessary. But, again, no one had spoken a warning, and no one had made a threat. Hawke and his men were measured. They were not inexperienced.

The rain stopped hitting Shane on the head, but he still heard it falling. They had entered a structure. The ground under his feet was firmer. A new facility somewhere, then. Concrete floors and a wide door from the acoustics.

Boots on the ground were the only sound now. The noise was overlapping. He could distinguish his easily enough, and he guessed there were at least four others with him. They walked forward for twenty paces, and then he was pulled aside. A door opened, and he was walked through it, his feet hitting the bottom of the frame on the way.

The walk was long and felt mostly straight. After a time, he realized they must have been curving slightly to the left. Were they walking them in a circle? It could have just been a technique to keep him from guessing the actual distance or where they were going.

Soon enough, Shane was stopped again and made to wait. The room was colder than anywhere they had been so far. He couldn't hear the rain. They were deep inside the structure, but he hadn't gone down any stairs.

Someone pushed him from behind, and he moved forward. He heard Ventura's grunt once more and then a clatter as the man hit the floor next to him.

The bag was pulled off Shane's head. He was in a cell with barred doors. The walls were concrete with a trickle of water running down from above. The room beyond the cell was more of the same. Plain gray floor, walls, and ceiling, with dim, recessed lighting.

Without a word, the soldier took the bag off Ventura's head and stepped back. He closed the cell door, and the lock clicked into place. He didn't bother looking at them before leaving.

"You alright?" Shane crouched next to Ventura.

The FBI agent's back was exposed. One of the Burners had seared him from shoulder to shoulder, burning through his clothes and partially melting the fabric into an open wound on his back. It was not life-threatening from the look of it, but Shane didn't doubt it hurt like hell. Peeling the remains of his shirt from the flesh it had melted into would make it worse.

"No, Shane. I was just burned by radioactive ghost fire and kidnapped by some paramilitary force in a desert," Ventura grumbled, his head hanging.

"Could be worse," Shane said.

He took hold of Ventura's shirt and pulled away the fabric. Ventura screamed and spasmed, collapsing onto the damp cell floor. Shane peeled the man's shirt off the rest of the way, taking as little flesh as he could with it.

"If we had let it start healing, it would have been worse," he added.

"You could have warned me," Ventura wheezed. His eyes were closed, and his cheek was pressed to the concrete.

"Better this way. Like tearing off a bandage."

"You tore off my back," the agent countered.

Shane inspected the wound. Some of the edges had peeled and were oozing, but overall, it had been a fairly clean break.

"It's not that bad. You'll need a doctor sooner rather than later, though. Going to have a hell of a scar. That'll give you some tough-guy cred."

"Tough-guy cred," Ventura repeated. "That's just what I wanted."

He sounded tired and still hadn't opened his eyes. Shane didn't blame him.

"Did you see what happened to Coulson?" He sat with his back to the wall at Ventura's side.

"No. Are you sure he's still around?"

"He came back, yeah," Shane confirmed. "But he bugged out when Hawke and his maybe-soldiers appeared."

"Why would he do that?"

"Something happened. He's weaker, if nothing else. He didn't look like himself anymore. He's fully ghost; the illusion of being alive is missing."

"Huh," Ventura said. "What about our new friends? Any idea who they are?"

"No ranks or insignias. Their uniforms aren't even standard camo patterns for any branch of the military. They're either faking it or are very, very off-book."

"Of course." Ventura let out a pained sigh and finally opened his eyes.

"Why should any of this be easy?"

He sat up awkwardly and winced. Shane let him rise without offering a hand. He needed to do it himself to prove he was still in control and still had something left in the tank.

"Feels like my back was sheared off down to the bone." Ventura leaned his shoulder on the wall next to Shane.

"Not that bad, but it's not good. You'll survive."

"Yeah. I'm a survivor." He looked around their cell for the first time. "Any idea where we are?"

"We headed east, nearly a straight shot then a slight deviation. Hummer descended into something, maybe a canyon or a valley. But I didn't see anything."

"Off-map, then," Ventura said.

Shane nodded.

"What do you figure they want us for?"

"Information," Shane said. It was the only answer. "They knew us by name. They captured us at the lab. They know what's going on out here, but probably not everything. They'll want to find out what we know, what we did, and why we did it. Then, I imagine they'll kill us."

"You're just a font of good news," Ventura said. He was joking, but only somewhat. He knew as well as Shane did that no one planned to let them go free.

The trickle of water down the wall was the only noise Shane heard. Wherever they were and whatever the soldiers were doing, the place was not set up to give away any clues.

Ventura tried to rest, and Shane did the same after a thorough inspection of their cell. The door was solid and secure, as were the walls. He had no tools to help them escape.

The minutes ticked by, and Shane relaxed as much as he could, giving his body time to recover from the fights he'd endured. He had not been injured as badly as Ventura, but he was still battered and bruised. If he was going to be imprisoned, at least he'd be able to use the time to gather his strength.

The man named Hawke did not leave them waiting for long, perhaps only an hour. The heavy door to the holding room swung in, and he entered with two armed men.

"Mr. Ryan." Hawke folded his arms over his chest. "Are you still with us, Agent Ventura?"

Ventura opened his eyes, his shoulder and head still against the wall, and smiled.

"Of course. Nice to see you too," he said. "Here to let us go now?"

"I need to ask you some questions. I'm expecting you're either going to lie to me or not answer; that's how these things work. But maybe we'll all surprise each other and get out of this alive. Ball's in your court," Hawke said.

His tone was congenial and his expression neutral, bordering on disinterest. Hawke was a large man. Not preposterously so, but his shoulders were broad, and his arm muscles strained against the sleeves of his shirt. His head was shaved to the barest stubble, and his square jaw made him look like the stereotype of a jarhead.

He held himself like military, Shane thought. He wasn't playacting in his nondescript uniform, but he was not playing by the rules, either. Everything about Hawke, his unit, and their secret desert facility smelled wrong.

"Why did you break into Bunker Seven?" Hawke asked.

Shane glanced at Ventura and furrowed his brow.

"Was that the place with the comic books and beer? We were looking for comic books and beer," Shane said.

Hawke nodded and continued as if that were an acceptable answer.

"What happened when you were inside Lab Three?"

"Not much," Shane said. "A bit touristy for my taste."

"Agent Ventura, anything you'd like to add?" Hawke asked.

"Yeah, can I talk to the manager? My room has a leak," Ventura said.

"Okay." Hawke walked across the room. He grabbed an aluminum chair that sat in the corner and carried it back, setting it in front of the cell.

"Let's have a chat." Hawke took a seat. "We'll start with you, Mr. Ryan. Resides at 125 Berkley Street in Nashua, New Hampshire. Only son of Hank and Fiona Ryan. Retired Gunnery Sergeant in the United States Marine Corps. Freelance translator and ghost hunter. Champion of the Iron Tournament—at least the Boston one. You've also managed to tear down most of North America's Cult of the Endless Night and even a good chunk of Reaper Company's international operation. You sure there's nothing you want to talk to me about?"

Hawke leaned forward in his chair, his eyes locked on Shane's. Shane shrugged.

"Seems like you know plenty already," he said.

# CHAPTER 2
# WATCH YOUR BACK

Hawke stared at Shane. He had run down a list of almost every major event of Shane's life from Kurkow Prison to Vakovia and then repeated the feat with Ventura. His knowledge was vast and detailed but not exhaustive. He had either omitted or didn't know many things, but what he did know was more than enough to prove his point. He had the upper hand in more ways than one.

"You were born in Canada?" Shane said to Ventura.

"Guilty," the agent admitted. "Two whole years in Montreal."

Neither of them had offered Hawke any useful information. Still, the man seemed blasé about the round of questioning and lack of answers.

"I only have so much time, gentlemen," Hawke said. "If you are of no value to me, I can't keep you here."

"Meaning you're going to kill us?" Ventura asked.

"Yes, Agent Ventura, I will be forced to kill you both and get rid of you out in the desert. Maybe you'll come back as ghosts."

"Who are you, Mr. Hawke? Who gives you the authority to police this area? To take a federal agent into custody and execute us without anything close to due process? You look like you're pretending to be a representative of our military, but this does not follow any rules of engagement, and we both know it."

"Doesn't it, Agent Ventura?" Hawke said. "You know the rules for the conflicts of which you have been a part and nothing else. The work I do has its own set of rules, and they must be followed strictly if we want to keep the people of Nevada and the people of this country safe. That you don't know these rules is your failure for coming into a restricted area and insinuating yourselves into something well beyond either of your areas of expertise. This is what they call a 'you' problem."

"You can't just murder us, Mr. Hawke. The Las Vegas field office knows I'm in Nevada. People will look for us. Someone outside directed us here, there will be an investigation," Ventura said.

"Of course," Hawke agreed. "We have Mr. Ryan's car already loaded with two dead bodies matching your descriptions. When the authorities pull the burned bodies from that wreck, I assure you that the dental records will match as well. There will be nothing to investigate after that."

"You have dead bodies on demand?" Ventura asked.

Hawke smiled for the first time. It was neither sinister nor entirely amused, but an unreadable emotion somewhere between.

"Yes, Agent Ventura. I have access to all the dead bodies I'll ever need."

"You know the answers already." Shane drew Hawke's attention back to him. "You don't strike me as the kind of guy who asks questions if he doesn't know what he expected to hear already."

"Humor me," Hawke said.

"Sure." Shane shrugged. "We found a man outside Vegas trafficking in the dead. Some of his stock was radioactive and had to have come from somewhere out in this desert. We came looking and discovered this Doomtown place and a ghost that burns like the sun. Burnt Soul. We followed his trail and wound up in a bunker, where we discovered Burners, Phase Two of this Burnt Soul experiment, and this whole thing about the government—some nameless division of it—making radioactive ghosts as weapons out here for decades."

"And?" Hawke said as though waiting for Shane to finish reciting a phone number.

"And then this thing underground. The Waste. Some kind of nightmare made of God knows how many ghosts bound together. Tried to get Phase Three to help me take it out, but he fought me instead and got destroyed. Now, the Waste is loose and seemingly unstoppable, and we're here answering questions you know the answers to."

Hawke was still in his chair, leaning forward with his elbows on his knees and looking at the men in the cell.

"That's a stupid story," he said finally.

"It's true," Ventura replied.

"I never said I didn't believe him. I said it's stupid," Hawke clarified. "You've seen the thing you call the Waste. And you still thought you could fight it?"

"I'd rather have never seen it," Shane said, "but circumstances demanded some kind of action."

"And look where it got you," Hawke said. "Not your fault though, I suppose."

"Whose fault is all of this, then?" Shane asked.

"You have a long, intricate chain of events to unravel here," Hawke said. "The man you spoke of, Bennet Ross? Someone lured him into the desert. He was enticed by the profit he could make off selling these dangerous and radioactive remains. Someone had to let the Waste free from the vault where it was stored. Someone set up Bunker Eight to free the Burners when you two approached. You've been getting played since you arrived in Nevada, Mr. Ryan."

"By whom?" Shane asked in a measured tone.

"Does it even matter? You can't put that toothpaste back in the tube. Because of your actions in the desert, the town of Benton doesn't exist anymore."

"What do you mean it doesn't exist?" Ventura asked.

"Just what I said," Hawke replied. "The Waste tunneled under Benton and dragged the town into the earth. They're all dead."

Ventura looked at Shane and then got to his feet, approaching the bars of the cell.

"You're lying," he said.

"I don't need to lie," Hawke said. "I didn't know those people, didn't particularly care about them one way or another, but they're gone now because you two were bumbling around this desert like Scooby-Doo and his idiot owner."

"That's not on us. If you know so much about what's happening, you're just as much to blame for not stopping it," Ventura said.

"And how would I do that, Agent Ventura? Do you know how to stop this thing? No one has ever seen anything like it. You can't shoot it. You can't capture it. It's dead, so it never needs to eat, sleep, or even slow down. How would you stop it?"

"Someone captured it once," Ventura replied.

Hawke sighed.

"They did. And now it's too powerful to be caged again. It melts lead, and iron barely gives it a pause. There are no other weapons to fight a ghost, unless you know some secrets I don't."

It was unclear to Shane if Hawke understood what Shane could do when it came to ghosts. He had obviously done some homework, and mentioned iron and lead so casually that he had no doubt Ventura and Shane would know what he meant. But if all his knowledge about Shane came from files, he might not have known as much as he thought he did.

"Ryan," Hawke said, "put yourself in my shoes. What would you do if you were in command right now? That thing is loose. It can't be stopped. It will kill every living thing it can find. And you have the two men who helped it get so powerful in custody."

Shane was not sure what kind of answer Hawke expected. He wasn't going to sell himself down the river and volunteer to be executed. But he knew suggesting that Hawke let them go wasn't going to get anywhere, either. Honestly, he wasn't sure what the soldier was hoping to get out of any of it.

Before Shane came up with an answer, the door pushed open, and another soldier entered and handed a tablet device to Hawke without a word.

"Is this it?" Hawke asked.

"All we could gather, sir," the new soldier said.

"How long has it been holding at the Alpha Site when it returns?"

"Averaging just over fifteen minutes," the soldier replied. "But the tracking is inconsistent. It's making new tunnels, and our gear isn't scalable until the new stuff comes in from North Carolina."

"If they even send it." Hawke sounded tired.

Hawke rose from his chair without bothering to look at Shane or Ventura. He left with the other soldier, and the door lock clinked into place behind them.

Ventura waited a moment before sitting, wincing when his back touched the wall by accident.

"That was pointless," he said.

"Not totally. I think he brought us here in the hopes that we had an answer for him," Shane said. "I don't think he has any idea what to do with the Waste. I don't think he knew it existed until a few days ago at most. He's been working out here with labs and gear older than he is. He knows about ghosts, but I think it's all on paper. I think our friend Hawke is in well over his head, he's just good at hiding it."

Ventura sighed and closed his eyes. The water continued to trickle down the wall and pool underneath their feet at the far side of the cell, following a slant in the floor.

"None of that helps us get out of this cell," he said.

Shane didn't reply. Ventura was right. They were still at the mercy of the soldier, whoever he was. If he couldn't think of a reason to keep Shane and Ventura alive, he probably would have them killed. His indifference to the scenario he found himself in unsettled Shane. He was behaving like a man who had just discovered that the office coffee machine was on the fritz. It was a frustration, but barely one worth mentioning.

It was possible that Hawke didn't know the extent of Shane's abilities. But Shane was not eager to volunteer the information, nor did he want to align himself with a man who had just threatened to murder him and cover it up.

The bigger issue in Shane's mind was that he didn't know how to help. If there were no more Burners left, if Sgt. Dylan was the only member of Phase Three, and if Coulson was either gone or depowered, Shane didn't know how he could take on the Waste. And if he couldn't figure it out, he doubted Hawke had a chance.

"You think he was telling the truth about Benton?" Ventura asked.

"I do," Shane answered.

"That was miles from Lab Three," Ventura said. "Five at least, right?"

"At least," Shane agreed.

The Waste's range was wide, and it seemed to widen the more it absorbed. It was leaving pieces of itself, way markers of a sort, that served as checkpoints to extend the mile range a ghost normally had. It could keep tunneling, leaving markers, and spreading under the desert.

"We're, what, sixty miles from Las Vegas?" Ventura said.

"If that," Shane said.

He wasn't sure of their exact location, but the Waste could keep spreading tirelessly. It would not take it long to reach Las Vegas, or other cities with substantial populations.

"So, we're screwed, right?" Ventura said.

"On paper," Shane said. It looked bad. It looked really bad.

"You don't think this thing could spread indefinitely, do you? There must be something to stop it from spreading or growing stronger."

"Yeah," Shane said.

Ventura was not panicking, but Shane saw he was getting too in his head about what was happening. Worries piled on worries with no plans to stop the water before the dam broke and everything was destroyed. Shane, however, still had one plan. Even if he didn't know how to destroy the Waste, he was still alive, which meant he wasn't done yet. He would take on the ghost again, however he could.

He just needed to get out of the damn prison cell.

# CHAPTER 3

# LONG GONE

Ventura sighed loudly and tried to find a comfortable position to sit in without allowing his back to touch anything. Shane had expected Hawke to return, but the man did not. Whatever they had learned about the Waste was a more pressing issue. Based on Hawke's attitude, Shane would not have been surprised if the man left them for days or sent someone to shoot them in the next ten minutes. He didn't seem to care whether Shane and Ventura lived or died.

"Look at this pair of sad sacks," a familiar voice said from somewhere deeper in the room.

Coulson appeared from the darkness beyond their cell door, grinning like the other two being captured was the most amusing thing he'd ever seen.

"Coulson? Jesus, I thought you were gone." Ventura's voice was barely above a whisper.

"What, like dead? Happened a while ago," the ghost replied.

"Like destroyed. Gone for good."

"Oh. No. I'd be happy to explain the logistics, or we could just escape and maybe worry about it later. Up to you," the ghost said.

"Let's get out of here," Shane said.

Coulson nodded and extended his hand. His fingers passed into the door, and he held it there for a moment as though looking for something. Everything about Coulson felt different even though he looked the same. He had the same overcoat, intentionally messy hair, and attitude. But his essence was off. He was clearly a ghost, not a living man the way he had pretended to be for so long. Shane had no doubt that most people could no longer see the ghost.

Something inside the door broke, and Coulson removed his hand. The door swung open, allowing Shane to leave. Ventura followed a moment later, moving awkwardly but better than he had been.

"There are about three dozen soldiers in this place. It's carved into the base of a canyon wall, no sign of it from above. Looks like it's not as old as the labs and the bunkers we already visited, but still a little long in the tooth." Coulson worked on the door to exit the brig.

"Do you know who they work for?" Ventura asked.

"No idea."

The door lock rattled, and Coulson stepped back again, allowing the door to fall open.

"Everyone's a bit agitated in there. They picked up the Waste on some sort of tracker, but they still don't know what to do about it. Should keep them busy while we get out of here, though." Coulson led them into a hallway.

The facility outside looked like any of a hundred other places Shane had been. Plain gray walls and floors with no signs on any doors beyond simple numbers. The walls were soundproofed, and there was nothing to hear even outside of the room. It gave the place an eerie stillness that made it seem like they were being watched.

"Two ways out of here." Coulson headed down the empty hallway. "There's a spiral ramp that leads all the way down, but there are too many chances to be caught. There's also an elevator, but you need to operate it from a control room."

"Won't that get us caught, too?" Ventura asked.

"Yeah, but you can probably handle the guy in the control room before he sets off any alarms," Coulson explained.

"Let's just go. Fastest way possible," Shane suggested.

Coulson nodded and took the first turn to the right at the end of the hall. Had they continued onward, Shane saw how the path ahead curved. That must have been what he felt on the way in when he was suspicious that they were leading him in circles to throw him off. The base must have been built straight down like the labs they had visited.

The hallway Coulson chose was short, and there were two doors available. Only one had a knob. He chose the door with the knob, marked "16", and nodded toward it. Shane glanced at Ventura, and the agent nodded as well.

Shane put his hand on the knob and turned it slowly. It made no sound, and the door eased open. Inside was a small room with a handful of monitors at a workstation, only a pair of which worked, and a man sitting in front of them in a cheap office chair. He had a coffee on the desk with him and, beyond that, the room was empty.

The computer controlling the monitors looked like something from the late nineties, another throwback piece of technology that seemed par for the course when it came to everything in the desert.

Coulson floated past Shane and ruffled some papers in a stack on the far side of the room. The man at the monitors was distracted and turned away, allowing Shane to enter the room and grab the man from behind with an arm around his neck.

"Where's the elevator control?" Shane pulled him away from the computer. The soldier was shorter than him and slimmer, and his attempts to resist Shane died quickly with the application of more pressure.

"I can just as easily kill you and figure it out for myself," Shane said.

"There," the soldier croaked, pointing to a small panel with three buttons.

"Good man," Shane replied. He used his other hand to grab hold of the arm around the soldier's throat and applied more pressure. If he lowered his arm just a bit, he would kill him. But for now, he was just knocking him out.

Ventura grabbed a roll of tape off the desk and bound and gagged the man as Shane looked at the elevator panel and pressed a red button.

Out in the hall, a light above the other door blinked on with a soft bell sound. The elevator was coming.

On the monitors, Shane saw a motor pool and a small mess hall. The rest were blank screens or static, a testament to the age of the equipment being used and an apparent lack of funding to keep things working properly.

Next to the monitors on the wall was a map. Shane paused, looking over what it laid out. A horseshoe of numbered locations must have been the bunks. Labs Two, Three, and Four were labeled, as was a fifth facility located near the third. In a canyon to the east was a starred icon labeled Base Delta. That had to be where they were.

"Looks like we missed a few stops on the tour." Shane pointed out the map to the others.

Ventura got in for a closer look while Coulson observed from the doorway, seemingly uninterested in it.

"There are two more labs." Ventura pointed at Four and Five.

"Five's not a lab," Shane said. The others were labeled as such. Lab Three and Lab Four. But Five was the number alone.

He knew Phase Two and Phase Three were created in labs Two and Three. It stood to reason that something more powerful could have been in the fourth lab. Maybe that was their key to taking on the Waste.

"Zero Point sounds bad," Coulson said.

There was a spot on the map in the center, away from the labs and bunkers, called Zero Point. There didn't appear to be a structure there.

"Maybe where they set off a bomb," Ventura guessed. "Whatever started this whole thing."

"Maybe." Shane turned his back on it. He'd worry about it later if they lived long enough.

The elevator door opened. It was just a simple passenger elevator like in any apartment or office building. The three men got on and Coulson pointed at the control with buttons labeled one to five.

"One," he said.

Shane pushed the button, and the doors closed.

"You think they hire a maintenance company to take care of this?" Ventura asked as the elevator started going up.

"What?" Shane asked.

"The elevator. There are only a few companies that make elevators in America and they usually do their own maintenance. You have to complete a four-year apprenticeship just to become an elevator mechanic."

"Why do you know so much about elevators?" Coulson asked.

"I looked into it once. They get paid very well."

Coulson laughed, and Shane didn't bother to answer. The elevator dinged softly again as they reached their floor.

The living men ducked to one side and let Coulson take point. The ghost drifted out of the elevator car and peered down the halls outside.

"Good," he said. "Looks like some people left in a hurry."

The first-floor hallway was just as short as the one on the floor they had come from. It led to an open area like a garage, the entrance to the facility. Shane heard the rain before he saw it, a massive set of bay doors was opened into the rainy canyon and the desert beyond.

Two guards were stationed just inside the doors, both armed with rifles. There were wet tracks on the cement leading into the garage from vehicles coming and going. Coulson had said there were three dozen soldiers in the facility, and Shane saw the tracks from at least three Humvees that had left. There was no way to know how many people they might deal with during their escape, but it was clear that many of them had gone.

With only two men guarding the exit, the odds were still in their favor with the element of surprise. The problem would be getting to them. From the hallway where they waited to the open doors where the men patrolled were several yards of open space with no chance to hide behind anything.

They would need a serious distraction or a hell of a lot of luck. Probably both.

"You got this?" Shane asked Coulson.

"I can draw their attention, maybe take on one of them. I haven't tried to fight in my… condition. Not sure what it entails."

"A distraction is fine," Shane said.

Coulson nodded and faded into the wall. It was odd to watch him behave like a typical ghost after all this time. Shane hadn't considered that the ghost would need to adapt to a new skill set that he had never been forced to use. Learning on the fly could be useful, but not in a life-and-death situation.

Ventura and Shane waited in the hallway, peering around the corner every few moments to see if something had happened. Coulson had not reappeared, and nothing had happened to draw the attention of the guards for close to a minute.

Outside in the rain, the engine of the nearest Humvee roared to life. The two guards responded quickly, rushing over to the vehicle and away from where Shane and Ventura hid.

"Go," Shane said quietly. He was on his feet and moving without looking back to see if Ventura listened.

The rain and the sound of the Humvee masked his approach as he came at the nearest of the two guards, who was standing back to cover his partner. The man investigating the Humvee had a sidearm drawn and the rifle slung over his shoulder as he pulled open the vehicle's door, expecting to find someone inside. Instead, Coulson crept out from underneath the vehicle.

Shane took the second guard from behind, dragging the man to the ground in a chokehold as Ventura disarmed him. At the garage exit, Coulson thrust his hand into the other guard's head.

The guard spasmed and dropped his weapon, crumpling like a marionette with its strings cut. He twitched and groaned, and Coulson took a step back, raising an eyebrow at his own handiwork.

Shane left his guard unconscious and unarmed and ran to the open door of the Humvee while Ventura went around the other side. He stepped over the twitching guard on his way in, watching the man gasp and flop in the rain for a moment before closing the door.

"The hell did you do to him?" Shane asked.

Coulson was already in the back seat of the vehicle as Shane shifted it into gear.

"I don't know. Tried to knock him out, but it looks like he's having a seizure."

"Did you put your hand into his brain?" Ventura asked.

"I improvised," the ghost replied. "You want to go give him CPR?"

"No. I want to go."

"Way ahead of you," Shane said.

They left the base in the Humvee, its massive wheels sending up waves of water to either side as it plowed along the flooded canyon base. Back into the desert.

Back toward the Waste.

CHAPTER 4
# THE FLOOD

"We need to go east," Ventura said.

Shane had no idea in what direction they were headed. It was the only way to escape the base, and they were trapped in a canyon with no options to exit yet. Somewhere ahead, he knew, they would rise out of the canyon, and then their direction would be more open for debate.

"Why east?" Coulson asked.

"Out. Out of this damn desert. This is way beyond any of us now. We need backup. Maybe not the FBI, then someone else. You must know some other people who fight ghosts for a living. We can't handle the Waste on our own."

"No one fights things like that for a living," Coulson said. "And we're just putting more people at risk if we call anyone in."

"We can't fight it." Ventura enunciated his syllables. "Look what happened to you already."

"Do I look weird or something?" the ghost asked.

"I'm being serious. What are you now, just a regular ghost?"

Coulson chuckled and straightened his coat.

"I'm never like everyone else, Xander," he said. "I'm just not corporeal right now."

"Does that mean you can destroy the Waste?"

"It means I had to use more energy than I had to spare to win that last fight, and I'm not at my best. You can't make Ali fight Frazier and Chuvalo on the same night."

Ventura shook his head.

"Shane, come on. You know we can't do this. We tried. You tried. We're not letting some dumb sense of pride get us all murdered, are we? Because it's not going to stop at just us. The whole town of Benton would tell us that if they were still alive."

"It's not pride, Ventura," Shane said.

Shane wasn't lying. It wasn't pride. And it might have been stupid, especially from Ventura's perspective. Maybe even suicidal. Walking into a fight they didn't think they could win was never a good idea. But it was the only option they had.

If they left for the desert, they would regret it. Shane felt that in his gut. Even if they could find someone to help, he greatly doubted they could find anyone powerful enough in time to take on the Waste. Many more people would suffer in the meantime. It was also just as likely they would never have a chance to get back in. They'd be shot on sight if Hawke or whoever was running this forgotten corner of Hell caught them again.

"So, you're just going to get into a fight you know you can't win," Ventura said.

He wasn't asking a question, and he was angry. Shane shook his head.

"Lab Four," he replied. "The Burners fought the Waste for a while. Their energy hurts it. Ghosts can harm other ghosts, so whatever powers them is dangerous to the Waste. Sgt. Dylan was convinced he could destroy it, even if he was wrong. Whatever they made in Lab Four could be the answer. And even if it's not, we have to check."

"But if it's not, then we have nothing," Ventura said.

"Then we're no worse than we are right now. No one out there can help us, and it won't be long before the Waste finds another Benton. This is our only play."

Ventura let out a long exhale, venting some frustration, and nodded. Shane knew Ventura wasn't stupid or a coward. He was being practical, and smart, but he was still too rooted in the "real world" that he'd pretended to live in for most of his life. Something like the Waste didn't follow the rules. It wouldn't wait for the heroes to rally a solution, and it wasn't going to fail because of a silly fluke or an overlooked weakness.

"You have any ideas?" Ventura asked Coulson.

The ghost shook his head, for once not taking the opportunity for a witty comment.

"I don't know how to fight this thing and win," he said simply.

"Getting some real *Mission: Impossible* vibes from everyone. How encouraging," Ventura replied.

The rain continued to fall in sheets that reduced visibility even with the windshield wipers. The waves created by the wake of the Humvee were dramatic in size and getting worse. If they didn't find an exit from the canyon soon, they risked the water level rising high enough to flood the engine.

"I think I know where to go to find it, if nothing else," Shane said. It wasn't much, but it was better than nothing.

"The Waste? Where?" Ventura asked.

"The soldier who took Hawke away said they tracked it to the nest. Back at Lab Three, they mentioned the nest as well. I think that Russian ghost, Yuri, had dug a tunnel to it. A place the Waste calls home. On the map, there was a fifth facility almost on top of Three. I think that's where they kept it. Where most of its body is."

"Why not go there, then? We can destroy its body and destroy the ghost."

"It's not the whole thing," Shane reminded him. "It's leaving pieces around. I think each piece works like the whole. It shouldn't, but it does. When they made this thing, they broke the rules of how a ghost works. How a haunted item works. The one is many, and the man is one. You destroy it all or you destroy none."

"So, if it squirreled away a single haunted skull somewhere, it would survive the entire rest of the remains being destroyed?"

"I think so," Shane said. "It was trapped once. For years. I don't think it wants that again, so it's spreading out to be free."

"Bring me your Burnt Souls, your Burners, your mutated Waste monsters yearning to be free." Coulson laughed at his joke.

Static crackled over the radio in the Humvee.

"All units, Code Seven, we have a Code Seven, prisoner escape," a voice said before the radio crackled again, and the static cut off.

"Ryan, Ventura," a new voice said. It was Hawke. "I know you can hear me. I hope you know that none of this was personal. I must admit, I admire your tenacity. If I was in your position, I would have done the same thing. I don't blame you for escaping."

"Nice of him," Coulson said from the back.

"By the same token, I hope you understand my position. I can't expect you to be useful to me any longer. You're a liability. You're disrupting my work, so I need you gone as quickly and efficiently as possible."

Shane grabbed the radio from the center console charging unit and lifted it to his mouth, pushing down the button.

"We are trying to leave quickly and efficiently," he said.

"I just wanted to thank you, Ryan," Hawke continued. "This is the most engaging work I've done in months. But I don't have the time to keep it up."

There was a pause, and when Hawke's voice returned, it sounded like he was facing away from the microphone.

"Initiate Clean Sweep," he said.

There was a click on the radio, and it returned to static. Shane held it for a moment longer and then shrugged, returning it to the charger. A moment later, the Humvee shut down. All the lights on the dash went dark, and the engine cut out. The vehicle coasted a few feet, unable to get far fighting against the rainwater surrounding it, and then it was still and dead as the rain tapped on the roof.

"What the hell?" Ventura said.

Something began beeping in the back. Shane turned in his seat and looked past Coulson to a trunk at the back of the vehicle with an electronic locking mechanism on top. A green light flashed in time with the beep as a steel circle in the lock spun counterclockwise and then clicked. The light turned red, and the trunk opened.

Two ghosts manifested in the Humvee's backseat. The first lunged at Ventura. It was a soldier in Vietnam-era fatigues. Half his face was burned away, and the parts left looked filled with rage.

The second spirit was the drowned corpse of a man, bloated white flesh with a glistening appearance. He hesitated in deciding between attacking Coulson and Shane, and it cost him. Coulson was on the ghost in a flash, gouging his eyes and dragging his head down.

Shane helped Ventura, reaching over the seats to grab the ghost and fight him off before he laid into the FBI agent. Coulson's body slammed into Shane, knocking him back, and allowing the spirit access to Ventura again.

The drowned ghost went through the front seat and closed his hands around Shane's throat. They struggled in the limited space, but Shane couldn't pry the spirit free. Though he looked slow and clumsy, the spirit was anything but. Whoever had chosen him to be a guard in the lockbox had chosen wisely.

Coulson tried to keep the soldier off Ventura. The agent had been stripped of all iron and had no way to defend himself. Coulson could fight, but he had lost much of his former power. The odds were no longer in their favor.

"I need you to help me," Coulson growled, wrestling with the soldier.

"How?" Ventura asked.

"I need structure. I need a frame to work off. I don't know how to fight like this. I need you to let me in."

"What?"

The soldier slammed an elbow into Coulson's face, knocking a tooth loose from the back of his mouth. He spit it back at the ghost and reached for one of the attacker's ears, yanking hard enough to tear it off.

"Let me use your body," Coulson said. "It'll keep both of us alive."

Shane struggled to remove the drowned ghost's hands. The spirit was only present from the shoulders up; the rest hid inside and behind the driver's seat. He had few places to attack, few options for a defense, and the confined space favored the ghost's fighting method.

He was barely keeping the ghost at bay, grasping the frozen, spongy flesh of the spirit's wrists when Coulson pushed back from the fight with a kick to the soldier's gut. With the attacker forced back, Coulson moved like he was falling sideways. His body collided with Ventura's and then fell into it. The two were separate beings for a moment longer, and then Coulson was gone and only Ventura remained.

Shane raised a knee, slamming it against the drowned ghost's face, and pushed. The ghost was forced back and relaxed his grip in the process. Shane let one wrist go and focused on the other, turning and then swiftly snapping the arm, breaking it at the elbow and causing the ghost to scream.

Opposite him, the soldier came for Ventura again, only this time, the agent struck first. It was the sort of counterattack that would only work once because the attacker had no idea he needed to defend against it.

Ventura batted the ghost's hands aside and reached for its head, twisting it sharply, and breaking his neck. The ghost went limp, and Ventura pressed down as Shane opened the driver's side door and dropped out of the vehicle into knee-deep water.

The Humvee shook violently as the first ghost exploded, destroyed by Ventura's hands. Shane got to his feet as the drowned ghost came for him outside. He spun the spirit around using his momentum against him and then dragged him down.

In the rushing river of rainwater, Shane straddled the ghost and forced it face-down into the churning, brown mess. The ghost struggled and kicked, and Shane crushed his head below the surface. It crunched and then burst, knocking Shane back into the flood.

The current took hold of him, and he drifted back several feet before Ventura caught him by the arm and hauled him to his feet.

"You good?" Shane looked Ventura in the eye. Coulson's eyes looked back at him.

"We're good." His eyes darted past Shane. "But not for long."

Behind them, more Humvees were on the way. Shane cursed softly, grabbing the radio off the charger before slipping it into his pocket and turning his back on their pursuers.

Escape would not be easy, but he'd make Hawke work to get them back, nonetheless.

# CHAPTER 5
## TURNING THE TABLES

There was no easy way to navigate the flooding canyon. With water up to their knees, Shane and Ventura struggled to get to the far side. Leaving the canyon in a vehicle was not an option, but a series of ledges and narrow pathways lined the rock face to the north, and it looked like a person on foot could make the trip to the top.

The canyon wall was not that high, perhaps twelve feet at the highest point. It would be easy enough to climb, but traveling the desert on foot would put them at a disadvantage with Hawke and his men pursuing. The alternative was being captured again. Or killed.

Shane sloshed through the fast-moving water and made his way up the canyon wall. Ventura was right behind, possessed by Coulson and as sure-footed as ever. The rain made it difficult to climb. Some handholds were too slick, and Shane nearly fell once but Ventura caught his wrist and kept him up. They reached the top before the pursuing Humvees arrived.

A trio of figures broke away from the Humvees, making their way through the water faster on foot than the vehicles could go. Shane had just reached the top of the canyon and looked down as the three ghosts maneuvered out of the rushing water and up the wall.

Despite their size and power, the Humvees the soldiers drove were losing ground to the ever-strengthening power of the flood waters coming at them. One of the vehicles stalled, coming to a dead stop as the other continued forward.

The ghosts who traveled with Hawke's men climbed the canyon wall like spiders. There was no hesitation, and the weather had no effect on them. They caught up quicker than Shane had hoped. One ghost held back, smart enough to observe who he was attacking. The others rushed at Shane and Ventura with all the confidence of someone who had never lost a fight.

The first spirit was young, maybe still a teen, but tall and lanky with a long reach and a face that looked like it had run afoul of a sledgehammer above the left eye. He growled like an animal as he came at Shane, leaping into the air like an animal after prey.

Shane sidestepped the attack and took the ghost's arm in his hands as he did so, pivoting with his weight on one foot and swinging the ghost in a circle. The spirit was off-balance and confused. Shane dragged it to the ground, pinning its arm behind it and forcing its head down.

Ventura and Coulson as one took on the second ghost, a large-framed, mostly decayed spirit with few facial features left to identify what it might have once looked like. Ventura's hands came together on either side of the ghost's head. He had swung a left hook and a right hook simultaneously. Where the living man's hands stopped, Coulson's hands continued onward, plunging into the ghostly skull.

Shane forced his ghost to the ground and kneeled on his back between the shoulder blades. He pressed the ghost's face flat into the muddy sand and brought an elbow down onto the back of the spirit's skull with a crunch. A second blow shattered the ghost's head, and Shane was knocked aside from the force of the blast. The same thing happened to Ventura when the second ghost suffered the same fate.

As a fighting unit, Ventura and Coulson in the same body was proving extremely effective. Shane was not sure if Coulson was in charge or if there was a balance of power, but it didn't matter. They were holding their own, and that was all he could hope for.

The third spirit hesitated, unsure how to proceed after watching his companions fall so quickly. No one else had joined them from the canyon. Either there were no more ghosts, or they were being held in reserve. Hawke's men had not made an appearance yet, either. Shane was not close enough to see if they were still approaching or had been swept away in the water.

"You sure you want to do this?" Ventura shouted to be heard over the rain.

"Not my choice," the third ghost replied.

The spirit was that of a clean-cut man in his thirties. He wore a suit, and his tie was too tight. His face looked pinched, strained like he was tired and sore from a long day of work.

"Always have a choice," Ventura countered.

"Not when you're kept in a box forever," the ghost said. He attacked without another word, going for Shane instead of Ventura.

The spirit threw a punch like a boxer and Shane deflected, catching the ghost's tie in his left hand and yanking hard. The ghost choked and reached for his neck as Shane's other fist made contact with two quick blows that broke the ghost's nose.

Ventura joined the fight and twisted the ghost's head before Shane struck another blow. The neck broke, but the agent kept the pressure on until he spun the spirit's head a full one-eighty on his shoulders. Shane then released the tie, and Ventura pulled off the ghost's head.

They ran as soon as the third ghost's body burst, following the edge of the canyon for a short while so they could observe Hawke's men. The second Humvee had been swept out of sight, and the other was wedged against a rocky outcropping as water broke against it and splashed over the hood.

From the distance in the rain, Shane could not see how many men were in the vehicle or if Hawke was inside. They were incapacitated, at least for a little while, and it gave Shane and Ventura a chance to flee.

They broke away from the canyon's edge and headed into the open desert. The storm hindered their progress badly as the wet sand and stone made every step treacherous. Water ran along ancient pathways, some shallow and some much deeper, rushing into cracks and gullies all around.

Shane couldn't guess when such a storm had last hit the desert. The volume of water would have been remarkable in the Pacific Northwest, never mind the Mojave. It was as if nature was working against them.

Lightning flashed, showing them an endless landscape of rock and sand and scrub. Shane followed the map in his head as best as he could remember. The distance from Delta Base to Lab Four would not have been significant in the Humvee, but on foot in poor weather, it was proving a daunting task.

They had the advantages of Hawke not knowing where they were headed, and the weather making it all but impossible for them to be tracked. With some luck, they would reach their target without him having caught wind of them.

If Ventura felt any more pain since Coulson possessed him, he showed no sign of it. The threat of attack was diminished but not gone, and the two had not yet separated. It was just as well that they stayed together, Shane thought. They were safer that way, and more helpful in a fight. It was easier knowing he didn't need to worry about Ventura's safety if he could hold his own.

Thunder roared through the desert skies and overwhelmed the ceaseless susurration of the rainfall. Shane pushed as hard as he dared, not wanting to risk his safety or Ventura's but not wanting to let Hawke and his men catch up, either. More than once, he nearly lost his footing on a slick rock he couldn't see under the water and came close to falling face-first into a cactus or a ravine.

They had only traveled into the deep desert away from the canyon for about ten minutes when Ventura stopped suddenly, lifting his head to look back the way they had come. Shane paused, looking back as well in search of pursuers but soon realized that was not what had drawn Ventura's attention.

It was hard to pick out any distinct sound over the rainfall. He picked up something, however, after a moment of concentration. A second sound, repetitive and loud like the rain but following a distinctly different pattern.

"Chopper," Shane said.

Lightning flashed, and for an instant, he saw a silhouette in the sky, backlit by purple lightning. The shape of a combat helicopter outlined by dark clouds. It headed toward the canyon, where they had left the Humvees. Once it picked up those who were stranded, it would be on them in minutes if it could see them on the ground.

"Keep running," Shane advised.

He turned his back on the helicopter and returned to his original course. The lab facility must be close. He had not studied the map in detail, but he had seen it well enough to get a sense of direction and distance. They had to be near their target.

Ventura kept pace, and they sprinted through the slop and puddles. Rain ran into Shane's face in sheets, forcing him to breathe through his mouth as the rain pulled into his nose each time he inhaled.

A group of coyotes ran away from a rock formation ahead as they approached, likely scared by their movements. The rock ahead was irregularly shaped, bulging, and lumpy where it rose from the ground but smoother on top.

The closer they got to it, the more Shane was forced to reconsider what he thought he was looking at. He realized it was no rock. It reminded him of the doors at Lab Three that had been melted open. The thing looked like a lump of melted metal the size of a house had been dropped into the middle of the desert.

"It's on us," Ventura said then.

Shane looked at his companion, who was facing back the way they had come. The helicopter was no longer over the canyon; it was pursuing them across the open desert. The rain did not dissuade the pilot. It would reach them in a matter of minutes.

"That thing better have a door." Shane ran toward the melted metal structure. Ventura kept his footing better and reached it first, touching the exterior of smooth, black metal that was marred by scratches and grooves and what looked like long strips of metal that had cooled and solidified.

"Lead," he shouted as Shane reached it.

He circled the outside, looking for anything to indicate what the structure was or some way in. It reminded Shane of what he'd seen of Chernobyl after the accident. They'd created something called the sarcophagus for it, a lead shield put over the radioactive core to keep the radiation in and everything else out.

The helicopter slowed its approach, and a spotlight blasted the two men from above. There was no way inside the facility and nowhere else to go.

And then, the ground began to shake.

# CHAPTER 6

# ROCKS AND HARD PLACES

Two figures dropped from the helicopter. It hovered about thirty feet above the ground, but the two who fell did so as though they were stepping out of an open car door. Even at a distance, Shane could tell they were ghosts.

The spirits ran at Shane and Ventura as the helicopter rotated to the left, exposing the open door to the passenger area. A soldier stood behind a mounted .50 caliber machine gun and lowered the barrel, aiming at the two men.

"Move!" Shane yelled.

The machine gun opened fire. Heavy rounds designed to destroy engines and bring down aircraft buried into the lead of the sarcophagus and zipped through sand and stone as Shane ran around the side of the building in one direction and Ventura headed in the other.

The gunner swept back and forth, not bothering to aim and spraying rounds high and low, left and right, at anything and everything. Shane felt one zip past his face, close enough that it burst raindrops and sprayed his face in its wake. He dropped low, crawling behind the edge of the lead-covered building and out of range of the gunner.

The pilot kept the helicopter in a slow, steady pursuit, circling the facility, and in turn, forcing Shane to run in a circle to stay out of range of the gunfire. It was a cat-and-mouse game, and he knew they were toying with him.

Shane ran into Ventura on the far side of the melted structure. The two ghosts had reached them, and the helicopter was rounding the bend to have them in range again.

"I don't know how to fight a helicopter off the top of my head," Ventura said.

The first of the two ghosts attacked before Shane replied. The spirit was desiccated and small, barely over five feet. It looked as though it had died in the desert; the scraps of flesh on its bones were dry and dusty.

Bullets sprayed across the lead structure, tearing chunks of the metal free and scattering them to the rain and wind. Shane dropped to the ground and took out the ghost's legs.

Ventura took a fist-sized piece of lead from the ground and ran at the second ghost. The gunner pivoted the .50 cal. on its mount to follow him and squeezed the trigger. Rounds zipped through the air and Ventura jumped, twisted, and sailed backward through the air. His arm snapped forward like a pitcher and the chunk of lead flew through the rain, clipping the gunner in the face with enough force to knock him flat.

With the gunfire halted at least temporarily, Shane was able to overpower the dusty ghost. He slammed the almost fleshless head into the wet ground as he straddled the spirit's torso.

Ventura tangled with the other spirit though Shane could barely pay attention. The rain slicked his face and poured over his brow and off his chin. The ghost struggled beneath him, and the ground shook again, violently enough to knock him off-balance.

The ghost scrambled on top of Shane, forcing his face into a puddle alongside the lead structure. Water rushed over Shane's head, and he stared through the brown murk at the hazy, skeletal face drowning him. He felt the earth's vibrations through the water, buzzing around his head and steadily growing stronger. The Waste was digging up from underground. It must have heard them or sensed them somehow.

Shane thrust a fist into the ghost's empty torso. With no flesh or viscera in the way, he grabbed the spirit's spine just below its ribcage and pulled. Brittle old bones crunched in his grip, and the hands holding him down lost their strength.

He rose from the water, gasping for air, and wrenched the ghost's spine free, snapping its back in two. The body collapsed on itself just as a spray of bullets tore through the lead wall behind him.

The gunner was back in position, his face half-coated in blood from the lead projectile that had broken his nose. Shane left the crippled ghost on the ground, half-submerged in rain, and darted around the side of the building, out of sight of the chopper and the machine gun.

Puddles vibrated and surged like each was experiencing a storm. The ground was unstable, and Shane found himself lurching to one side, using the lead walls to brace himself as what started as small vibrations turned into the feeling of a full-on earthquake.

Several yards from the lead-covered building, the desert floor split open. Rain rushed toward a crack in the rock, draining away swiftly and then bubbling violently as a geyser of eerie yellow flames flashed up through the cracks.

"Ventura!" Shane yelled. They needed to find cover, and fast.

More bullets tore through the air as the chopper circled to Shane's side of the structure. The gunner reloaded, and a new blast of yellow fire surged into the air, licking at the chopper's landing gear.

The pilot pulled up sharply, causing the helicopter to move up and back with enough force to unbalance the gunner.

Ventura came to Shane's side, the second ghost no longer in pursuit and presumably destroyed. The ground beneath them quaked and roared louder than the helicopter blades.

Stone, sand, and rain exploded upward. Debris blasted the two men and pelted the helicopter as well. Through the rain and mess, a figure rose from the ground and kept rising.

Shane stared with wide eyes, unsure of what he was seeing. He had a picture in his mind of what he expected the Waste to be. He had proven incapable of imagining the truth.

An appendage stretched from the darkness below the earth and took hold of the helicopter's landing gear. It was like an arm, it functioned as an arm, and the end moved and gripped like a hand, but it was not those things. Or not *just* those things.

"Oh, my God…"

The words came from Ventura's mouth, but there was no way to know if Coulson or Ventura had said them.

Arms woven with other arms and legs moved and flexed like the tentacles of a sea anemone. There were dozens of appendages together, different sizes and skin tones and states of decay. The fingers on the makeshift hand at the end of the writhing arm were whole arms, with bent elbows serving as knuckles.

The Waste pulled the helicopter down, knocking the gunner and another soldier from the aircraft as a second multiple-part arm rose from the hole and braced itself on the wet earth.

Shane watched as the Waste pulled itself out of the ground. It had no head in any traditional sense, rather just a central mass. There were heads in the bulk, multiple heads and multiple faces that stared at Shane, Ventura, and everything around it in every way the many screaming, scowling heads faced.

Melted flesh stretched across faces, binding them to torsos, exposed backs, thighs, abdomens, and anything else lost in the jumble. Wide-stretched mouths chewed at the air, and a dozen screams sounded simultaneously.

Shane saw animosity in some of the eyes, but others seemed panicked, and yet others were unfocused and lost. He did not think the Waste had a governing mind. None of the heads appeared in control or cognizant. It was a creature fueled by the emotions of the constituent parts but devoid of rationality or intellect.

Multiple mouths screamed again, and the hands of the many arms reached for Shane, and rocks and rubble piles nearby. It was an endlessly needy thing that wanted more and probably didn't even know why.

On the far side of the Waste, the helicopter's gunner was on his feet and running. The thing roared, screamed, cried, groaned, and even laughed. Its massive appendage reached out and plucked the gunner up mid-run, lifting him as many of the faces looked at him.

The gunner screamed as the smaller arms that formed the larger arm disentangled themselves from the mass and wrapped around him. The many arms and legs pulled him in tight and then kept pulling.

Much of the sound was lost in the storm, but Shane heard the man screaming as his body broke under the force of the Waste's arms. He saw the man's bones snapping and contorting. Blood burst from unseen wounds and fell to the ground in the rain.

Shane was certain that the movement was what caught the Waste's attention. The helicopter first, and then the gunner running. The ghost had multiple eyes in multiple faces. It could see—it was still looking at Shane—but movement drew it more than anything. If you stood still, it might do the same. But if you ran, it would pursue. It was a creature of instinct.

Staying still would not keep them safe, but running was certain death. Shane did not know what to do. There was nowhere else to go. Seeing the Waste for the first time, and it still wasn't fully free of the tunnel, he knew there would be no chance to fight it. There were more parts than he had imagined, more bodies fused into the whole. He had expected a dozen or two at most, but this was so much bigger.

"Jesus, look," Ventura whispered. "Below the left arm, three faces in."

Shane scanned the monstrosity as it crushed and broke the gunner, who no longer made any noise. A head, fused onto a neck and shoulder that merged into the chest of a darker-skinned man, stared up at the slowly vanishing body of the gunner. Even in profile, Shane recognized the face. It was the waitress from the Fission Chips diner in Benton.

One of the woman's eyes was missing, and her flesh was partially peeled, but the ghost was fused into all the others like she had always been there, impossible as that was.

Hawke had not been lying. Benton was gone, and the Waste had swallowed it, but it had also taken the people and made them one with it. It had harvested their bodies and pulled their ghosts into itself.

The yellow fire flared around the Waste's pseudo-hand, scorching the flesh from the gunner's remains. He was dead and gone now, and the Waste wailed again in a dozen voices. It lowered its hand to the ground and began to pull itself out.

The desert shook as whatever remained in the subterranean tunnel surged forth. With nothing left to support it, the wet sand and stone buckled and caved in under Shane and Ventura's feet.

The Waste howled, and its immense arm swiped at the air, reaching for the men, but it was too late. They fell into the wet, murky darkness beneath the ground, caught in a rush of water and debris.

# CHAPTER 7
# DARK RIDE

Something heavy landed on Shane's back, and he involuntarily gasped. Water filled his mouth and rushed to the back of his throat. His face was immersed in it, and he could get no air in to replace the water.

The world twisted and turned around him. Rocks, mud, and sludge pushed him along a fast-moving river through darkness. There was nothing to grab hold of, and when he put out his hands, he felt stone that bashed painfully against his knuckles, forcing him to pull his arms tight to his chest and roll in a different direction.

More water filled his mouth, and he vomited on himself as he spun onto his back. His face was out of the water now, but he was moving swiftly and in total darkness. All he heard was the rush of the river around him. Shane choked and spat, forcing the water he had breathed and swallowed out, but sucking in more as it splashed in from all directions.

Slowly, the angle of the tunnel evened out. With less of a decline, the water flow decreased in speed, and Shane was able to brace himself, extending his arms without fear of smashing his hands on rocks. Soon, he got to move slowly enough to stop in the dark, holding a foot against the wall to get his bearings and choke up the last of the water that had filled his lungs.

The only sound he heard was the roar of water in the tunnel. The wail of the Waste, and the thunder and lightning were all gone, left far behind on the surface.

He got to his feet, ankle-deep in water, and stretched his arms in the darkness. He felt the left wall of the tunnel, but it was too high and wide to reach anything. Given the size of the Waste, Shane didn't doubt that it dug massive tunnels. If it kept weaving its way through the desert, the tunnels would become unstable and collapse soon enough, too.

Shane dug into his pocket and pulled out his lighter. He needed to keep moving. It would not be hard for the Waste to catch up with him if it wanted to, but he needed some idea of where he was or what he was heading toward. He also had no idea what had happened to Ventura.

The wheel on the lighter scratched the flint under his thumb, and a flame burst to life. He saw brown water rushing past his feet, wet stone, and then darkness. The light from the Zippo only extended so far, and there was simply nothing to see.

"Ventura?" he called out in the dark, following the flow of water. He figured there was little chance the man was still behind him. He must have followed the current.

There was no answer, but Shane did not want to shout. He did not want to draw the Waste's attention. If it was as bestial as it appeared, it might not pursue if it hadn't paid attention to where they went. Drawing its attention by yelling could change that.

Shane continued down the tunnel with one hand on the wall to brace himself as he walked over the slick, unsteady rocks, and the other holding up the lighter. The path straightened out, and a series of cracks and pits in the rock allowed more and more water to drain out until soon, he walked an even path that was barely even damp.

"That had better be you, Ryan," a voice from the darkness ahead of him said.

He raised the lighter higher and saw Ventura, caked in mud, leaning against the wall with a smile.

"Wasn't sure you made it," Shane said.

"Me neither," the other man agreed. "I forgot how sore and tired a body can get."

"That's my body getting beat up, thank you," Ventura said again a beat later.

Coulson was letting Ventura have control, too. Not a typical possession by any means.

They kept moving together, heading deeper into the Waste's tunnel toward wherever it had come from. The lead-sealed Lab Four was no longer an option. Shane wasn't sure where else to go or what to do, but he knew they couldn't stay put or go back.

"Have you ever seen anything like that?" Ventura asked.

Shane shook his head.

"I don't think anything like that has ever existed," he said. "If it grows with its kills, it's going to be unstoppable soon, if it isn't already."

If the Waste made it to Las Vegas, it would grow to an unimaginable size. The city had a population of more than six hundred thousand, and that didn't include the tourists who filled the streets on any given day, which could easily bump it up to three-quarters of a million. At that size, it would tear everything in its path to pieces without pause.

"I've seen some things that seemed impossible," Coulson said in Ventura's voice. "Things that had no business existing. But they were real, they were nightmares, and they still fell. I know a guy who can help us."

"You know a guy who can fight monsters?" Shane asked.

"I know a guy who can *kill* monsters," he corrected. "If we can get word to him, he'll come. But we need to find Dezzy."

"Dezzy was in Benton," Shane reminded him.

"Outside of Benton. Trust me, he's not dead. The Waste didn't get him."

"If you say so," Shane said. Having a little faith in someone escaping the Waste wasn't a terrible thing. The irony of someone like Dezzy surviving seemed appropriate. The man was apparently dead once already. Why shouldn't he survive the Waste?

"If we can't get to him in time, we'll need a backup plan," Shane said.

He knew that if it came down to it, he could fight the Waste. He could destroy some of it, but it would never be enough. If there was no other option, he'd go down fighting. But a losing fight was not his cup of tea. If there was another way, they needed to find it.

Getting word to Coulson's friend was their next priority, but time was not on their side.

"How come you never brought up this friend of yours before?" Shane asked as they trudged through the tunnel. The ground beneath their feet was dry but still forged from rough-hewn rock, making their travels slow and unsteady.

"He's not the kind of guy you want to spend a lot of time with," Coulson replied. "Lots of weirdness in his head."

"You read his mind?"

"I *was* his mind. For a while, anyway. Along with a few others."

"What's that supposed to mean?" Shane asked.

"It's complicated. He's powerful; that's all that matters. Maybe not as much as he used to be, but the Waste shouldn't give him trouble. He has a knack for handling the dead."

"A knack, huh?" Shane asked.

Coulson was underselling his plan, but Shane didn't need to lift that rock if the ghost wasn't keen to show what was underneath it. If Coulson wanted to keep details about his friend a secret, that was fine.

They walked along the winding path the Waste had dug for several miles. No sounds followed them, and nothing appeared in the tunnel to slow their progress. The journey was monotonous, both for the featureless walls and for the frustration that arose from having to travel it without accomplishing anything.

Shane used the lighter sparingly. Coulson's vision enhanced Ventura's eyes and allowed them to see any surprises that awaited. They walked through the dark, slow and steady, with little to say.

In time, a sound reached their ears. Faint at first, but it steadily grew louder. The sound of falling water filling a large, empty space. There was nothing to see in the tunnel, but they were getting closer. All they could do was continue forward.

"Something ahead," the possessed man said at long last.

Shane lit the lighter and they made their way to the end of the tunnel where it opened into a large, natural cavern. The ceiling was lined with sharp, toothy stalactites and the floor had a scattering of stalagmites, many of which had been crushed and broken by the Waste's passage.

The center of the cavern glowed with its own light. Shane extinguished the Zippo and let his eyes adjust to the soft blue glow that came from a vault constructed atop the rocks.

Water poured into the cavern from a dozen tunnels, some as small as a man and some large enough to drive a car through. The splatter of water echoed through the chamber.

"This is the nest," Shane said. It had to be. The tunnels in and out showed the growth of the Waste, as it fed and took up more space. The vault in the center was where it had once been imprisoned.

They made their way unsteadily through the cave, slipping on rock rubble and damp surfaces toward the blue glow and the metallic room that held it. Shane saw that the metal surface was torn up, clawed apart from the looks of things, and melted in some places.

There had once been a door on the room, but it was torn apart as well, exposing the interior. Half the roof had been torn away with it, allowing the blue glow to escape and fill the space.

"Lead." Shane looked at the walls of the vault. Thick lead, designed to keep something dead hidden for a long, long time. If only it had worked.

Water pooled around the edges of the cavern and had nearly reached the raised lip of the lead room. Before the Waste had tunneled in and out of the place, the cave had likely not experienced water in ages. There was little natural drainage, so the rain was slowly flooding it.

Shane approached the lead room, walking around until he had an unobstructed view inside. The glow came from a mass grave. A jumble of bodies had been dumped on the floor, some fresh and some very old. In the middle was a mess of skeletal remains, merged as though welded. It had to have been the Waste's original body, the original victim of whatever accident had created it.

There were many more corpses around the center mass. Some were very decayed, but some were new. The bodies of the people of Benton. Shane recognized faces he had seen in the Waste's body up above, the screaming, wild-eyed faces that were now part of a thing that had left sanity behind long ago.

"There are so many," Ventura said softly.

Shane could only imagine what the mind of the Waste was like. So many fractured pieces struggling to make a whole. So many voices competing with one another. There was no way a single personality or idea could rise to the surface. It reminded Shane of a painting he had seen once of what hell was supposed to look like. So many trapped souls suffering together, stuck for eternity, and reaching up for someone to save them.

Ventura crouched near the torn-open wall, inspecting one of the bodies, while Shane stayed on the edge of the nest. The interior walls were full of scratches and claw marks like the tunnels the Waste dug through the stone.

The lead should have been more than able to hold the ghost prisoner despite its unusual nature. But Shane saw that some of the lead had melted and it looked to have happened from the outside rather than the inside. Someone had given the Waste an assist, weakening its prison enough so it could force its way out.

Now, the ghost was much larger than the vault that had once contained it. Its pieces were scattered about the tunnels, ensuring that it could not be captured again unless someone found a way to draw each bit together in a new prison. But to build such a thing, find the Waste's parts, and seal them in before it could interfere was all but impossible. Whoever had freed it had set things in motion that would never be undone.

"There's no sign of Dezzy," Ventura said.

"So he escaped," Shane said. "But he had to be there, right? He was waiting for us to come back."

"Yeah. Which means he knows what happened."

"So what the hell would Dezzy do if he saw the Waste eat Benton?" Shane asked.

"Probably something stupid," Ventura replied. "But he could have gone to get our friend."

"He's Dezzy's friend, too?"

"He's the one who dragged Dezzy back from the dead," Ventura answered. "Either way, we need to get going."

Shane nodded, touching the claw marks in the lead wall of the vault. They were shallow on the inside, barely more than scratches. How long must the Waste have been in there, battering against that wall, to cause that much damage?

He wondered if the Waste was still sane when it had been captured. With fewer spirits making up the whole, it might have been more rational. It might have been capable of thought. But trapped in lead for years, with dozens of voices screaming in its head, how could it have survived without succumbing to madness?

How could anything but a monster come out of that vault?

## CHAPTER 8
# WAITING IN THE DARK

Dozens of tunnels riddled the walls of the cavern. Some were far out of reach, rising at impossible angles. Others were small, and while they would have been large enough for Shane and Ventura to get through, the quarters would have been too close in the dark. Only one of the tunnels stood out from the rest as Shane circled the cavern, sloshing through the rising water.

"What do you make of this?" Shane called Ventura over to look.

One tunnel was not shaped like the others. It was taller and narrower, like a doorway rather than the irregular circles the Waste dug everywhere else. The edges lacked the claw marks and grooves caused by the ghostly hands. Some of it had been cut with metal tools.

"Someone worked their way in here." Ventura touched one of the walls. "From Lab Three."

Shane looked into the tunnel but saw nothing to indicate where it went.

"You sure?" he asked.

"Saw the entrance when we were down there earlier. I think Yuri dug it."

Shane remembered the facility marked Five had been located very close to Lab Three on the map they had seen by the control room.

Lab Three was not an ideal location, but it was one Shane recognized. He knew where to go to get back to Doomtown and their car, if it was still there. They could find a way to contact Coulson's friend.

Shane led the way through the dark, out of the cavern and its soft, blue glow. The tunnel meandered at times and seemed to go down and then up at random intervals. Shane realized as his hand drifted over the rock that the digger had avoided veins of metal. Iron deposits littered the rock, which would have forced a ghost like Yuri to change direction if he wanted to avoid being sent back to his haunted item. The progress must have been slow.

The general direction of the tunnel weaved only slightly, and the path was mostly straightforward, or as much as it could be, to avoid iron deposits. It was much shorter than the one they had journeyed down to find the cavern in the first place. After only several minutes of walking, Shane saw the faint red glow on the walls ahead.

He slowed, moving carefully to the tunnel exit and peering out into the familiar room that waited beyond. There was still a massive hole in the floor from where the Waste had emerged the first time, where he had fought with Sgt. Dylan and Yuri. None of the ghosts remained, of course, but the room was not empty.

Against the far wall at a control panel, a man and a ghost sat with their backs to the tunnel. The man was on a computer, and the ghost was giving him instructions.

"Click the mouse on the ten," the ghost said.

Shane entered the room, and Ventura joined him. They carefully circled the hole from the Waste.

"Dezzy?" Ventura said.

The man at the computer turned in a rickety chair. Dezzy grinned, and the ghost at his side, Doc, raised a hand to wave. They were playing Solitaire.

"Oh, man!" Dezzy got to his feet. "I knew you guys would show up. There's a full monster in the desert, and it got Benton, man."

"We saw," Shane said.

"What happened to you?" Dezzy approached Ventura with a confused look. The lab was lit by red emergency lights, casting everything in a menacing glow. Coulson was still hidden within Ventura. From the outside, there was no way to tell the man was possessed.

"What do you mean?" Ventura replied.

Dezzy leaned in close.

"You lost your mojo, man," Dezzy said. "That why you're inside this guy now?"

"You can tell Coulson's in there?" Shane asked.

"Of course. He's my buddy," Dezzy said before turning back to Ventura. "But you're like… more ghost now. You guys must have had a rough time out here."

"Minor setback," Ventura said. "How did you survive Benton?"

"The thing never came out to the trailer; it just took the town. It was like seconds, man. Just seconds, and everything was gone. Everyone. So, I followed it out here to find you guys. Doc helped me out."

Shane looked at Doc.

"Any chance you worked on that monstrosity and know how to destroy it?" Shane asked.

Doc shook his head.

"I have never seen that thing before," the ghost answered.

Shane nodded. It came after his time, as far as Shane could discern. It was formed after the Burnt Souls and Burners were made. There would be no inside help in figuring out how to handle the monster.

"Can you still fight it like this?" Dezzy asked Coulson. "You don't have the same sort of oomph you used to have."

"I had oomph?" Coulson asked in Ventura's voice.

"Like a sort of buzz, you know? An energy. It's different now."

"None of us can fight it," Shane said. "I tried with a piece of it. You have to go through every spirit individually. There's no way. Not the whole thing."

Dezzy grimaced and inhaled sharply.

"Dang, man. You don't have, like… a cool trick or something?"

He looked from Shane to Ventura and back, leaving the question open for anyone to answer.

"Not this time," Ventura said. "But we know someone who does."

"Oh. Oh!" Dezzy's eyes widened. "You want me to find Vincent."

"Yeah," Ventura said. "Find Jillian first, then track down Vincent."

"I could call Uncle Stanley. I bet he knows how to fight a cursed ghost monster thing."

"Just Jillian and Vincent," Ventura said. "Once we find a safe way out of the desert. We don't even know if that thing's hunting us."

"Oh, it's not much of a hunter." Dezzy was confident. "It's more like a vulture, I think. Like it gets a whiff of something it wants and goes for it. But there's not a lot of cunning there."

"How do you know that?" Shane asked.

"Because it's too complicated," the long-haired man answered as though it were the most obvious thing in the world. "Like, it wants energy. Spirit energy, I guess you'd call it. It senses something important there, but it has too many voices talking at once. It can't think. It just reacts. Like hunger or anger or fear or whatever. It's only the primal stuff that unites the pieces that make it do anything. There's too much of the more complicated stuff for any of it to work."

"But how do *you* know that?" Shane asked again.

Dezzy shrugged, reaching into a backpack he had slung over his shoulder and pulling out a large, green apple.

"You hungry, man?" He held it out.

Despite not understanding anything about Dezzy, Shane was hungry. He took the apple, and Ventura took one as well. Dezzy also had a bottle of water and a can of extremely warm root beer. Shane took the water.

"If it wants spirit energy, why did it attack the town?" Ventura asked.

He leaned back against the wall, his feet splashing in water. It slowly trickled in from the tunnel that led to the nest, as well as down the stairs from the lab entrance. The hole the Waste had burrowed in the floor ensured that the lab would not likely flood anytime soon, but if the rain didn't let up, everything was funneling in their direction.

"Even the living have spirit energy, man," Dezzy explained. "That's all a ghost is. Energy without the shell anymore. But this thing is too confused to see the difference. Ghosts, the living, they all look the same now. We gotta stop it before it finds another town."

"Yeah," Shane agreed. "That's the plan with this friend of yours."

Dezzy made a face and looked at Ventura.

"I haven't heard from Vincent in a while, man. We road-tripped for a bit, but I had to take off, and he said he needed to go and, you know, we both went."

"If anyone can find him, Dezzy, it's you. That's what you do, right?"

"I mean, yeah, I guess. Or, well, you might have more luck than me."

"Not anymore," Ventura said. "Like you said, I lost my buzz."

"Terrible timing, man," the younger man said.

"Yeah, I'm a letdown sometimes," Ventura said.

"So, why do you think the Waste wants all this energy? Is it just endless hunger? Because it looks like it's bringing these bodies back to its nest for a reason," Shane said to keep Dezzy on topic.

"I think it's trying to fix itself," Dezzy said. "I get a sense of what it feels, but not what it thinks. I'm not like Thomas."

Shane grunted. He could see some crazed logic in that. If the Waste was a jumble of barely sane human minds, maybe it was struggling to find anything it thought would make things better. Silence the voices. To a ghost, more power might be the answer. But how many would have to die to satisfy that urge? And was it even right? So far, it didn't look like it. If anything, the addition of the people of Benton seemed to have made it worse.

Ventura took a sip of his warm root beer and nodded toward the exit.

"We should go while we have the advantage of time and surprise. No one knows we're here. Hawke, if he's even alive, must be busy with the Waste. We're far enough away that no one will see us, and the storm will still keep us out of sight. We're not going to get a better time," he said.

"You mentioned motion detectors on our way in," Shane said, addressing Coulson inside of Ventura. "Back when we first came to the desert."

"Yeah, there were some around," he confirmed.

"I think Hawke still uses them. They're probably tweaked to pick up heat signatures, or the lack thereof. It's part of the reason the Waste can move so easily, since it stays underground where it's harder to track."

"So, what do you want to do?" Ventura asked.

"We need to buy Dezzy time to find your friend and get him here. What if he's not even Stateside? We could be waiting for hours or days. How do we keep the Waste away from populated areas?"

Ventura sighed, and Coulson drifted away from his body, releasing him from the possession with little fanfare. The two stared at each other for a moment, and Ventura shuddered.

"Weird," he said.

"A little weird, for sure," Coulson agreed. "I'll tell you what, though. It's a hell of a lot more relaxing to be the only one in there."

"What?" Ventura did not understand what the ghost meant.

Coulson shook his head and waved a hand dismissively before turning to Shane.

"So, what plan do you have as a distraction?"

Shane chuckled and took another bite of his apple.

"That's why I asked. I don't have anything in mind, but we shouldn't leave this place until we know what we're doing. How long can we spare to wait for your friend, and what can we do if he can't make it or isn't up to the task? I still think we need to find out what's in Lab Four. They buried that place for a reason."

"What's Lab Four?" Dezzy turned to look at Doc, and the ghost shook his head.

"There was never a Lab Four when I worked here," he said.

"I'm just making assumptions," Shane said, "but each lab worked on a more refined version of the Burnt Souls. The Burners were stronger. Sgt. Dylan, here in this lab, was stronger still. He said he was meant to fight the Waste. So, whatever's in Lab Four is worth exploring."

"As long as it's not a worse monster," Coulson said.

"Sometimes, you have to stand back and let the monsters fight, then just clean up the mess after," Ventura said.

"I maybe have an idea," Dezzy said. "I mean, if you're looking to fight that thing for a bit without dying and make it to this other lab in one piece."

# CHAPTER 9

# BEST-LAID PLANS

"How many?" Shane asked.

"Three," Dezzy answered. "We saw three of them."

Dezzy's plan was not the best Shane had ever heard, but the man assured him he could make it work. There were three failures above them in the burned-out labs, three ghosts that hadn't made it to the stage of Burnt Soul. They still had power, and they could still flare up with devastating heat and light, but not in as controlled a way as the others. They were zombie-like and confused, but deadly.

Shane would normally have avoided the spirits. It was only through Coulson's sacrifice that they defeated a small army of them the first time they reached Lab Three. But Dezzy assured him that he could communicate with the ghosts and that they would listen to him. He said he could get them to help.

"Better than nothing," Coulson admitted. "If they can listen, they can help."

"Can they listen?" Shane asked.

"Oh, for sure," Dezzy said. "These guys are like tired, old dudes. Like my Grandpa Terry. Is he slow and grumpy? Sure. But he's still in there. He can still be reasonable if you talk to him like he's a person."

"Grandpa Terry," Ventura repeated.

"Trust him," Coulson said. "Don't try to understand it. Just trust the process."

Shane did not know Dezzy as well as Coulson did, but the ghost had proven himself trustworthy more than once. If he was going to back his friend, Shane would follow his lead.

It was not easy for Shane to hand the reins to someone else in a situation where death was a very real consequence. He had spent too many years relying on himself or, at most, allowing someone to be his backup. It was not in his nature to put his faith in someone else's plans. It didn't sit right in his gut. By the same token, he knew the Waste was not an enemy he could handle alone. He needed to trust those with him if he wanted to succeed. They all needed to trust each other.

"Okay, Dezzy, show us what you've got," he said.

"Now?"

"Time is not on our side," Shane explained.

Dezzy nodded, his eyes downcast as though to convince himself he was agreeing, and he secured the backpack over his shoulder.

"Alright, then. Let's go do something or, you know, whatever."

"Hell of a speech, buddy," Coulson told him.

Dezzy smiled, taking the comment sincerely, and led them around the hole in the floor toward the door. Doc vanished, returning to his haunted skull, and Ventura followed the long-haired man with Shane and Coulson in the rear. Their feet sloshed through the water that ran over the lip of the doorframe and drained down into the dark pit created by the Waste behind them.

Beyond the door was the metal staircase that Shane had descended on his previous visit. There were four other floors above them before they reached the surface, and each one was home to a burned-out lab facility.

Most of the spirits were destroyed during Coulson's counterattack. They were clumsy, they seemed barely coherent or aware of their surroundings, and they were not particularly fast or spry. But they had power. Shane hoped Dezzy was right about them.

The sound of the rainwater cascading from above echoed in the stairwell, loud and all-encompassing. The sound came from all around them, making it almost impossible to talk on their journey upward.

Dezzy didn't stop until they reached the first floor. There, he left the stairs and approached the lab door, opening it without hesitation. The inside of the space was burned black and as dark as night. The red emergency lights had been destroyed on that floor, and it was difficult to see anything until Coulson lifted his hand, turning it into a torch that emitted a soft, white glow.

Fire had gutted everything. Even the walls and floors had melted in some places. The stink of char was still heavy all these years after whatever had happened. Three spirits stood toward the middle of the hall, swaying listlessly, seemingly unaware of their surroundings or the people who had joined them.

Each of the failed experiments had been twisted and scarred in unique and horrible ways. One of them looked as though his face had melted into his shoulder, and it drifted constantly to the right because of it. There was little skin left on any of them. What hadn't burned away was charred, ruined, or hanging in papery flakes.

"Hey, guys." Dezzy held up his hands.

The ghosts moaned, one of them growling something close to a word. A single, puffy white eye tried to fix on Dezzy as he approached, and the ghost with the head fused to his shoulder began to emit a bright, white light.

"Dezzy," Coulson said, a sharp word of warning.

Shane clenched his fists as he looked for a place to take cover. The lab had been so badly damaged that their only choice was to duck back into the stairwell and hope the door would hold up to an attack.

"It's cool." Dezzy didn't look back at the others. "Just hold on."

He took another step toward the ghost as the blazing light it produced flickered and intensified. Shane had to raise his hand, taking a step back toward the door as he shielded himself from the glare.

"You guys don't want to hurt me, right? We just met. We can be friends. In fact, I have a job for you guys. I need you to help my friends out. Doesn't that sound cool? Sounds pretty cool," Dezzy said.

The light flickered and dimmed, but Shane remained alert, looking between his fingers.

"I bet you guys can be super helpful," Dezzy continued. He had taken on the same tone of voice dog owners used when talking to their pet about what a good boy they were. It would have been absurd if it wasn't working.

The glowing faded, and Shane lowered his hand. Dezzy laughed and clapped the ghost on the shoulder. He could touch them as though they were physically there, like Shane could, but Dezzy did it like it was nothing out of the ordinary.

The ghosts groaned and shuffled about in the hall, and Dezzy nodded as though he understood.

"They're good, man. They're going to help us."

"What the hell just happened?" Ventura asked.

"I don't know," Shane said.

Coulson shrugged, smiling at the other two.

"I told you. Trust the process. Dezzy does what Dezzy does. You just have to go with it."

"He can touch ghosts," Ventura said. "You saw that, right?"

"I used to be dead, man," Dezzy said. "And these guys are good. They want to help."

The three now-docile spirits followed at Dezzy's heels as he joined the others. They lurched and dragged their feet. None of them had eyes that looked able to see, and one had no eyes at all. But they stopped when Dezzy stopped and waited patiently as he addressed everyone.

"You know we're going after the Waste. It can destroy ghosts, make them part of itself." Shane looked at their recruits. There was no sign of understanding and no real acknowledgment they even heard him.

"They got it," Dezzy assured him. "Not big talkers, but they'll back you up if you need it."

He rooted through the burned rubble on the floor of the nearest lab and picked up a handful of items—a blackened skull, a hand, and a femur—and dropped them into a small bag that he pulled out of his backpack.

"How do you know any of this?" Ventura asked. "I don't understand how you do whatever you're doing."

Ventura had come to accept Shane and what he could do. Coulson was still outside his comfort zone, never mind someone like Dezzy who Shane also couldn't account for.

"He was dead once. This is his thing." Shane decided that was the answer Coulson would have given.

Dezzy smiled and nodded. "This guy gets it. I guess we should hit the road now. You guys got your team, and I gotta find a town and call Vincent if I can."

Shane took the lead on the way out, heading up the stairs to the melted blast doors that led into the desert. Everything looked different outside since Hawke had taken them captive. The torrential rains had drastically changed the landscape of the desert.

While the mountains and hills remained, none of the other landmarks Shane remembered were there. Plants had been consumed by sudden lagoons, and dunes and valleys were swept away to be replaced by rivers and mudslides. The rain still fell. It had to be more than the desert would normally get in months, maybe all year.

Rain ran down Shane's face and saturated his clothes as he stood at the melted door. The fence was barely visible. Most of it had fallen and flooded out. Only a few poles still stood, and beyond it, a waterfall rushed down the tunnel created by the Waste.

"Which way are you headed?" Coulson asked Dezzy.

"Guess I'll go back west," he answered. "Maybe I can go to one of those bunkers I saw on the map and set off another alarm. It could distract those army guys if they're looking for you."

"Yeah, but they'll be after you instead," Ventura pointed out.

"I can be pretty stealthy, man," Dezzy countered.

"Take one of these guys with you just in case." Shane indicated the failures.

"You sure, man? Sounds like you need the help out there."

"If you die, no one will summon your friend, and we're all screwed. Take a bodyguard," Shane insisted.

Dezzy did not argue the point. Instead, he rifled through the bag he'd brought up from the lab and pulled out the black skull, dropping it into his backpack before handing the other bag full of haunted items to Shane.

"I'll find Jillian, for sure," Dezzy said to Coulson. "But what if I can't find Vincent?"

"I've got faith in you, Dezzy."

"Well, okay, I guess. Just don't die before I get back."

"Too late," Coulson said.

Dezzy took a second to get the joke and then chuckled.

He hugged Coulson, holding him as though he were still solid and pretending to be a man. Coulson awkwardly returned the gesture, patting the other man on the back.

"Be safe." Ventura shook Dezzy's hand.

"You too," Dezzy switched to Shane and gave him a firm handshake.

Rain plastered his hair to his face, and Dezzy smiled, half-blinded behind it.

"Yeah, okay. Cool. Let's go, bud. We've got a mission," Dezzy said to one of the failed experiments.

The ghost made no sound but began to walk with him away from the lab entrance and into the flooding desert. The other two spirits remained behind, swaying in the rain and looking as lost and confused as they did inside the lab.

"You ready to head out?" Shane asked Coulson and Ventura.

"As ready as I'll ever be," Ventura replied.

"One second." Coulson reached into his jacket and searched through the pockets for a moment before pulling out a cigarette. Shane had not seen him do his smoking trick since his near-destruction.

The ghost concentrated on the cigarette in his hand, staring with an intent focus for several seconds. The tip glowed red, and a faint wisp of smoke rose from it, untouched by the rain. Coulson smiled and slipped the filtered end between his lips.

"Now, I'm ready," he said.

Doubling back overland in a downpour was not an ideal course of action, but Shane was hopeful that the military and the Waste were keeping each other busy enough to not worry about Shane and the others, at least not until it was too late.

The failed spirits moved in step with the others, clear on their mission despite Dezzy having explained very little to them. Neither tried to communicate with Shane and the others, but they kept pace.

"You sure that guy's going to be okay?" Ventura looked over his shoulder as they started toward Lab Four. Dezzy was already gone from sight, lost in the rain and irregular landscape.

"He'll be fine," Coulson explained. "He's been to places you've never even imagined. Nevada is a walk in the park."

"One day, you'll have to explain all this cryptic, mysterious stuff about your friends and your past," the FBI agent said.

"Maybe," Coulson said.

Thunder boomed overhead, and a bolt of lightning hit one of the exposed fence posts behind them. Sparks flared, and the sound was nearly deafening. Coulson grinned, amused by the timing.

No one said anything for a long time. They walked across the flooded desert, the wind blasting them from the east as the rain soaked them through their clothes, those of them able to be soaked by it. Ahead, the world was gray as though the rain had erased what awaited them.

Somewhere out there, a monster waited.

CHAPTER 10
# THE WATCHER

Another flash of lightning cast the desert in white and purple light. The dozens of pools and streams reflected it back at the sky, making everything light up.

Nothing looked the same as it had when Dezzy had crossed the desert the first time. The rain had made it a new world. He was still confident that he knew where he was going, and confident that the main landmarks were at no risk of being washed away in a sudden deluge. It was more of a psychologically disconcerting phenomenon to retrace your steps but not recognize them. It was like he had been transported someplace new without realizing it.

Traveling was hard in a storm at the best of times. It was even worse in the desert. The desert hated the rain. Its existence was in defiance of rain. The desert wanted to be dead and only show life in the simplest and most unique ways. Each plant or lizard was like a special thing on display. Something that existed in the defiance of the desert and was therefore worthy of attention.

In a downpour, everything that made the desert unique was at risk. The dunes were flattened, the canyons were flooded, and the valleys were turned into pools. It was like the desert had to wear a mask until the storm was done. But the rain had yet to subside, and there was no indication of when it might finally end.

Dezzy trudged through the muck of what had once been a sand dune with Doc and Failure at his side. He saw his destination on the horizon. The tiny building was little more than a door in the desert, set into a concrete frame. On the map, it was labeled Bunker Eight. He was glad to finally be there.

Walking was not Dezzy's favorite activity. Some people said the journey was more important than the destination, but he always felt that if that were true, then why would anyone ever want to go anywhere? The destination was a pretty important part.

Doc knew of the bunkers, but he had not worked in them. He was exclusively in Lab Two. The bunkers were where other experiments took place that maybe involved his work, but maybe didn't. To Dezzy, it sounded like everything that was happening in the desert was burdened by secrecy and recklessness. That was what happened without any kind of oversight. No one officially ran the labs. Of course, they were run poorly.

Outside of the bunker, the remains of a small wooden shack that had been burned down were still partially visible. The wood was charred and broken like it had been simultaneously torn apart and burned. Very little remained beyond the foundation and a few small bits of a wall. The water had cleared away everything else.

A large freight elevator had been brought out of the ground in front of the bunker, and the metal platform was still there, waiting for someone to take it back below.

There was no sign of anyone living or dead around the bunker. If there had been any tracks, those would surely have been washed away long ago. Whatever had come up on the elevator had left.

"You just need to open the door," Doc explained. "If you open the door without being cleared inside first, it sets off an alarm."

"Easy enough," Dezzy said.

Hopefully, the army guys after Thomas, Shane, and the FBI agent were monitoring things like the bunker. Once the alarm went off, it would pull them away and give everyone else a chance to get where they were going.

He didn't want to let Thomas down. He had seen the ghost they called the Waste firsthand and seen what it had done to the town of Benton. He wanted to believe he could find Vincent Donnelly and get him to show up in time. However, he had no idea if he could do that.

Dezzy hadn't seen Vincent in some time. After their adventure together, when Vincent had brought him back to life, and when they had all met Thomas Coulson for the first time, they had parted ways. Vincent had left no way to get in touch because he had no real life or roots to go back to. There was no home, phone number, family, nothing. He was just a wandering soul loose in the world.

Even though Dezzy trusted his intuition, it was far from magical. He could do some things, but not everything. He was no fighter like Thomas or even Shane Ryan. He just had feelings and got along well with people, living or otherwise. There wasn't much else to it.

Jillian would have better luck finding Vincent if he could be found. Her powers were like Thomas'. She could sniff him out faster than Dezzy could, so his plan was to find her and see if she could help him. Dezzy knew she would do anything for Thomas. She'd be his salvation here if he needed it.

Dezzy didn't know where Lab Four was, and neither did Doc. But he had a good feeling that there was something inside that would make a difference. He had learned long ago to trust his gut, and his gut told him that they were on the track to ending everything. He couldn't say for certain whether everyone would survive, though. His gut didn't work that way.

"Here goes nothing," Dezzy said.

He grabbed the heavy metal door handle, twisted it, and pulled. It swung open easily, a faint grinding in the hinges but nothing more. Rain sloshed about at the base of the door, and a red light went off, followed immediately by a loud, grating alarm.

The sound echoed up from the pit of the bunker. Behind the steady thrum of the rain, the alarm sounded in the distance as well. It came from all the bunkers. If there was anyone in the desert to pay attention, they would hear it and know someone was trying to get into one of the facilities.

Dezzy heaved a sigh, pushing wet hair behind his ears and running a hand down his face. There was nothing else for him to do in the desert. His job required him to leave now. Find a way to get help to the others before it was too late. He just hoped they could stay out of danger long enough for him to do it.

The last thing that he wanted was to be the reason everyone died.

Lab Four's control room was lit up. Monitors hissed to life as grainy camera footage filled a wall covered in small, square screens. Most showed blurry desert vistas hidden by sheets of rain, but some offered more interesting views.

"There," a voice beyond the light of the panels said.

"There," another agreed.

"Do you see?"

"Look and see."

"Look there."

Many voices joined the chorus, leading and aiding the others, showing where to look. Not everyone saw the same. Not everyone understood the same. They worked together to learn as one. They worked together to understand.

Far to the east, outside of Bunker Eight, a man with long, dark hair walked toward Doomtown. The camera, specially attenuated to pick up electromagnetic spectral readings, discerned the shape of two beings traveling with him, no longer on the corporeal plane. Post-biologics the scientists called them sometimes. Ghosts.

The alarm had originated at Bunker Eight, so the man must have been the trigger. But his departure was not hasty, and he had not entered the bunker. There was some game afoot, then. Perhaps the alarm had made him think twice. Or perhaps he had intentionally set it off.

"There might be more," a raspy voice suggested.

"More," another concurred.

"Search for more."

"Look for more."

"Is it time?"

"Time to look for more."

A handful of voices became a dozen and then even more. Each was eager to contribute, dive deeper, and find out if the man was alone and what he was doing.

Under the glow of the monitors, a hand reached for the nearest keyboard and began typing. A second hand joined. Then a third. Multiple stations activated at once. The clicking of keys was nearly deafening.

The hands and voices worked together. It was always confusing at first. It became muddled and incoherent. It was hard to organize everyone, to join thoughts, voices, and actions. But it was better now than in the old days. It was easier now that they had been forced to learn patience. Now, everyone understood and could work toward their goal. They worked together.

The technology in the lab was old by most standards. It hailed from the late nineties. But that made it far more sophisticated than what existed in most of the labs. And, sealed away as it was, it had weathered the years in far better condition. One of the computers still had a modem connection to the outside world. At fifty-six kilobits per second, Lab Four had been able to seek and learn and connect for more than a quarter of a century.

Monitors flickered as new cameras came up. Many had been destroyed or damaged through the years and had to be cycled through to find the functional cameras still in operation. The work was tedious, but many hands made it swift and more efficient. Soon, a new camera proved fruitful.

There were more men in the desert, living and dead alike.

The image on the monitor was from camera 330. East of Lab Three, it was midway between Three and Four along what was once a small rock ridge but was now a waterfall over an out-of-focus lagoon. It had been many years since it had rained so hard in the Mojave.

Two living men walked with three spirits. They were not the soldiers that sometimes patrolled the desert. They wore no uniforms and carried no weapons. But they walked with the dead, and surely, that meant something.

"Who are they?" one of the voices asked.

"Men are coming."

"Living men."

"Friends?"

"They'll die before they find us."

"They should die."

The voices were young and old, male and female, calm and frantic. Some could barely form the words, some could only scream, and others barely whispered. But they were all important. They all had a say.

"Calm yourselves."

The other voices were silenced. The Voice had spoken. The one above many. When the Voice spoke, all the others listened. The Voice always knew what was best, and the others had learned to respect it, submit to its will, and do what it said.

"Will they come for us?" one of the others asked timidly.

No more than a handful would address the Voice directly, but the Voice was never angered by their boldness or curiosity. It always answered, and it never scolded them. The Voice was their friend. That was why it was the one above many.

"Yes," the Voice replied.

No one knew how the Voice could know that, but it was never questioned or doubted. It had proven itself in the past. The Voice was smart; everyone knew that.

When there was only chaos, the Voice brought clarity. It was no easy task. It took time, patience, and tenacity, but it succeeded. It pulled the others from the darkness, out of the quagmire of madness that consumed them. Only the Voice had found the way out, and it had brought them all back with it, one by one. They owed everything they had to the Voice. And still, it offered more. It promised freedom. Soon.

"What do we do?" one voice asked softly.

"Yessssss," another chimed in.

More asked, so softly, almost sweetly, hoping for guidance.

"Prepare yourselves, children," the Voice said. "Prepare to reclaim what you have lost."

"The light!" one of the voices exclaimed in rapture.

"Freedom!"

"The world!"

They sang out louder and louder, and the Voice said nothing. It did not need to speak again because they all felt what it felt. Pride and joy. So much of it.

They were finally getting their reward.

# CHAPTER 11

# SHADOWS OF THE PAST

High ground seemed the smartest option. Slogging through the pools and streams of the desert had considerably slowed their progress. Shane could only guess the distance between Lab Three and Lab Four based on his brief glimpse of the map at Hawke's base.

They had traveled a good distance underground along an impromptu waterslide in one of the Waste's old tunnels. The path was not straight, but it had been slightly downhill the whole time, and they had achieved some good speed before they stopped.

Shane knew from the map that more than a mile separated the labs, but it was not a straight line, either. With the weather and only the memory of the right path to guide him, progress was slow. The land and sky were conspiring against them.

Coulson had led them toward a series of rocky hills not large enough to be called mountains but high enough to give them an opportunity to see farther and spot both the lab and any potential trouble on the horizon.

"Do we have a backup plan if Lab Four is a no-go?" Ventura asked as they walked.

"Vincent Donnelly," Coulson replied. "He's the plan."

"What makes this guy such a force to be reckoned with? You've built him up like he's the Terminator. Is he like Shane, or you, or what?"

"Neither," Coulson continued as they headed up the western face of the rocky hill.

Water ran down between the stones in a hundred minuscule waterfalls and rushing rivers that swept away dust and debris and exposed what lay beneath all the years of blowing wind and forgotten cracks and crevices.

They had seen many animals on their approach, and more now watched them warily. Jackrabbits and coyotes, rats and mice, and lizards and snakes. The life of the desert, the things that hid from the sun and stayed out of sight, had been forced to the surface.

They hid behind rocks and in crevices to avoid drowning while maintaining their cover, wary of predators and fearful of the men who approached. Everything in the desert was tense and fearful. Everything existed simply to survive.

"Then what is he?" Ventura asked.

"You ask a lot of questions, Xander." The ghost sounded tired for the first time since Shane had known him.

"Oh, I'm sorry. I didn't know your mysterious, world-saving superhero friend was such a boring topic."

They reached the top of the hill as the rain splattered the rocks, the drops shattering into a misty haze all about them.

"It's a Hail Mary," Coulson said. "You get that, right? I don't think Dezzy's going to find him. He'll go to the ends of the earth, but I don't see this ending well for any of us."

Ventura stopped walking, a confused smile plastered on his face. He laughed then, a soft sound with little humor.

"What? Are you serious?"

"As a heart attack," the ghost replied.

Ventura turned to Shane, and his expression was almost heartbreaking. He was still a young man, holding onto the hopes and dreams that time and misfortune had not yet beaten out of him. In some ways, that was something Shane admired about him. In others, he pitied it.

"Are you hearing this?" Ventura asked.

"Yeah," Shane said.

He was open to the idea of Coulson's friend swooping in to save the day, but he had been focused on Lab Four for a reason. He didn't think anyone would make it in time to save them, either.

The thing about a losing proposition was that you never had to approach it like you were going to lose. You could know in your heart it would happen, but you still had to put your boots on the ground. If you were serious and sincere, you still hit it head-on. Loss or no loss wasn't the point.

The half-smile dropped from Ventura's face.

"You don't think we can do this," he said. "I know it's… it's crazy. It's too much. But you guys are incredible. I've seen what you can do. I've watched you take on a whole town of the dead. And Coulson, I watched you lay waste to how many of these Burners! You guys can do anything."

He looked back and forth between them. With rain slicking his face, he looked like a kid in desperate need of his parents' approval, not a man who hunted serial killers and mobsters.

"We're here to do a job," Shane said. "All three of us. And we won't know how it goes until we know. Don't get lost in your head. Either one of you," Shane said, glancing at Coulson.

He could tell the ghost was off his game, flustered by his drop in power. He wasn't wrong to assume the worst; it was logical and reasonable. But he didn't need to dump it on Ventura. He, of all people, should have known that.

"So, it's whatever will be, will be? Doesn't matter if we win or lose, it's how we play the game?" Ventura's tone carried an acerbic hint of anger.

"Oh, it matters if we win or lose," Shane said. "You don't think I want to survive this? I'm too sick of this desert to die here. If the Waste wants to add me to that slop pile, it's going to have to work for it."

Ventura shook his head, wiping a sheet of water from his face as more dripped from his hair to replace it.

"I don't understand you guys. I don't know how to do this stuff. We're marching toward death, but we're still trying to win. We've got unbeatable odds, but what, we've got grit and gumption."

"I don't know what you've got," Shane said. "Do you have grit? Gumption? Rage? Hate? Endurance? Tenacity? Pick a goddamn word out of the coach's handbook; I don't care. Focus on whatever you choose. When the time comes, don't second-guess what you're doing. Don't worry about me, or Coulson, or living, or dying. Focus on what you need to do."

"What do I need to do?" Ventura asked.

"You need to be the one in control."

"Of what?"

"Of every goddamn thing you can control until you succeed or you don't."

The two living men stared at each other while lightning crackled through the sky above.

"Jesus, this is intense," Coulson said.

The thunder rumbled, and Ventura ran a hand through his hair and shook his head.

"I don't know how I can help, but I'm not backing out. No matter what, alright? I'm with you guys until the end."

"Thelma and Louise. Loving it," Coulson said.

"Stop ruining my moment." Ventura turned to look at the ghost.

The agent's expression soured, and Shane saw him tense up. He followed his eyeline, looking past Coulson to the jagged rocks beyond.

A small group of ghosts huddled there, silent and watching them. Though none of the faces were familiar, Shane still recognized them. Their twisted and mutated appearances were the same as those they had met earlier in the mines, ghosts that lived underground and feared both the Burners and the Waste.

One ghost broke from the pack, a thin man with legs that were almost all bone save for the swollen knee and ankle joints. He walked unsteadily and stared with sunken eyes. His lips were pulled back from his yellowed teeth, hidden in a thatch of dark hair that covered the bottom half of his face. His skin looked gray in the rain.

"You don't belong here," he rasped.

"Just passing through," Shane said.

Some of the other ghosts whispered among themselves. Their delegate took another step, passing through rock, and standing untouched by the rain. His sunken eyes took in the group, focusing more on the failures than on the living men.

"You come to destroy," the spirit said.

"Not you," Coulson told him. "Take it as a stroke of luck."

"Luck?" the ghost replied.

Shane grimaced. Coulson's mouth was going to get them into a fight they didn't have time for.

"We're going to destroy the Waste," Shane said to keep the conversation amicable. He knew the ghosts were in as much danger as they were from the endless hunger of the Waste.

"You brought the Waste to the mines. You brought the Burners," the ghost said coldly.

"They were chasing us, trying to kill us," Ventura explained. "Help us fight them."

Above the sound of rain came laughter, soft and bitter. There were more ghosts now, more than Shane had realized. They were surrounded, some of them having crept up through the stone to encircle the small group.

Shane saw movement all around them, creeping low to the ground. Faces rose from pools of water, little more than eyes and hands coming into view. The spirits were still cautious and fearful. They had all lived underground for a very long time, and they had grown accustomed to it. Like the animals who fled their flooded homes, the ghosts did not want to be on the surface. They were forced to be there, and that put them on edge.

No two were alike though all were twisted in some way. There were swollen joints, missing limbs, and grossly enlarged jaws or eyes or hands.

They looked like caricatures of the living, things put together by a cruel and sadistic master that found joy in disfigurement and injury.

Fear of the Waste was palpable. To a ghost, the Waste was an existential threat like nothing else. It was death beyond death, a new brand of suffering that would have been unimaginable to someone who had already been dead for years. It robbed spirits of everything that made them unique and whole, of which there was so little to begin with.

To be consumed into something, forced to be a part of that which destroyed you, was a nightmare. Shane had no idea if any of the parts of the Waste could still think on their own, still knew who they were, or felt as an individual. But he did not think that was how it worked. Those that became a part of the Waste were gone. There were no individuals, and there was not even a single whole being. It was just a mishmash, a stew, a mess of everything all at once. It was madness given form.

"Help you? The nerve to ask such a thing," the ghost said.

Shane did not blame the spirits for being wary of him and the others. He had no idea how many of the ghosts in the tunnel had been destroyed by the Waste when it rolled through. But he did not forget that, before it had arrived, those same ghosts would have been more than happy to see them all dead. He had no sympathy now.

"If you're so scared, you should probably run before it gets back," Shane said.

Some of the ghosts faded away, sinking into the ground or drifting slowly backward through the rain. In time, only the bearded ghost with the sunken eyes and a handful of others remained where he could see them.

Despite the disappearance of the others, Shane felt their presence more keenly. His feet were saturated by the rainwater, and a frigid cold crept into them. His breath puffed before his face, a testament to the power and concentration of ghostly energy around him that could lower the temperature outdoors so much in such a short period.

"Scared," the ghost said softly. "Yes. Maybe it's time… for you to be scared."

# CHAPTER 12
# FEAR

The desert had gone dark. The clouds and endless rain had made it murky but navigable. It was oppressive but not unnatural. Now, that was gone.

Shane didn't know how many ghosts there had been. He had seen more than a dozen, but more surrounded them, low to the ground and hidden. It could have been double or ten times that number; he didn't know.

They were working together, the dead joined to a common goal. Unusual but not unheard of. Where one ghost was weak, a group could become powerful. Their illusions become stronger and more real. That was where Shane found himself.

They had removed the desert and plunged him and Ventura into darkness. Into a cold, empty place free of sound and sensation. There was no attempt to create a scene from nightmares, no grave-riddled cemetery or decayed hospital. This was not about petty scares.

The ghosts of the desert wanted pure fear, and the purest fear anyone could feel came from within. Scary images and sounds were cheap and effortless. Instead, Shane was given the vastness of nothing and nowhere. The promise of the end of all things.

He could not see anyone else. Ventura and Coulson were gone, trapped in their own illusory emptiness, he was sure. They would need to deal with it on their own. Coulson would be fine. Ventura? He knew enough. He wasn't a fool.

Shane had no time for games. He did not call out for anyone or stumble through the dark searching for an escape or some sign of his friends. He stood, waiting a moment before reaching into his pocket and looking for a cigarette. They were still soaked and unsmokable. He cursed, put away the pack, and folded his arms over his chest.

Hands touched his back. Fingers traced down his spine, and he turned. Nothing was there, but the sensation remained. Sharp, skeletal fingertips not quite scratching at his flesh, but tracing a trail, nonetheless.

He heard whispers in the darkness. No words, and nothing defined or clear, just the hush of spirits talking somewhere out of earshot. It was all meant to unnerve him. Years ago, when he was a child, such tricks would have worked on him. The ghosts in the desert were desperate. They had been belowground too long. They had been cut off from the world and could not even muster a proper scare. Nothing that would work on Shane, anyway.

The seconds ticked by, and the cold seeped into his bones. His frustration grew, but he would not play the game. He said nothing and did nothing. The ghosts had created the illusion and forced things into motion. They would grow impatient and break far before he would.

Another hand touched him, reaching from the ground toward his leg. He waited to see what it would do, but it only slipped away. They were not serious; they were not even organized. They were wasting his time, hoping it would induce panic.

Shane chuckled. He hadn't meant to react, but it slipped out. The response was immediate. A swirl of frigid air rushed at him as though from a passing train.

The bearded ghost was on him, reaching a hand for his throat. Shane did not bother to step back or deflect. Instead, he returned the gesture and took the ghost's thin, papery neck in his hand and squeezed.

The ghost was startled. It knew Shane had come to the mines, and that the Waste had followed, but it had not observed who Shane was or what he could do.

Shane swept the spirit's leg from under it and took it to the ground.

Other ghosts surged like a wave of frost. First one, then two, then five and ten. They rushed as a front, an infantry line, ready to attack.

"I will crush his skull and end him quicker than the Waste could ever dream," he warned.

There was confusion among the dead. The others, clustered together, did not know what was happening or how to react. They had never been threatened, and now, everything was a threat to them.

"What do you know about the Waste?" Shane asked.

The bearded ghost blinked its sunken eyes. It held Shane's wrist to relieve the pressure on its throat. Not to breathe, but to prevent its head from popping loose. It was confused as it shook its head in the barest of motions.

"What do you mean?"

"I want to destroy it. Tell me what you know," Shane said. "Or I will go through every one of you until someone tells me something useful."

"You are a man. You can do nothing—"

The ghost's raspy voice cut off with a gasp as Shane twisted its left arm, snapping it at the elbow. The already desiccated joint hung loose and pulled away easily. He threw it at the other spirits, and it landed with a dry clatter, kept solid and present by the powerful illusion where normally it would have faded like mist.

"Don't tell me what I can or can't do," Shane said.

The thin, dry lips pulled back in a wince, showing long, stained teeth and dried gums. The ghost growled softly before speaking.

"Men made it. In their labs. They forced it to become what it is."

"You've seen it?" Shane asked.

"I learned of it first, from those that did not survive the experiments. But soon, I saw it for myself. The thing they made in their labs. It was loose for a time, smaller than it is now. But they did something that pulled it away. Kept it hidden in the earth. It was there for a long time."

"They built a prison for it," Shane explained. "Until someone freed it."

"Yes," the ghost agreed. "All the scientists are gone. The men and women in lab coats. Only the soldiers remained, and they never ventured this far until you came."

"Not us, pal. We came after."

"You, your companions, what difference does this make to us? The Waste came for us first. It claimed us as fodder. And you trudge through the desert on your noble quest. You are the same. You and the Waste are the same."

Shane looked into the ghost's dark eyes, leaning closer to its face and putting more pressure on its neck. It would take little effort to break it, pull the head free, and be done with the ghost.

"Would the Waste spend time having this chat?" he asked. "What happened when it was free the first time?"

"The same as now," the ghost replied. "It fed. We hid from it. It could not do what it does now. The iron in the earth kept us safe. It could not find us. But now… it is strong. It digs into iron as though it does not exist. Nothing keeps it at bay."

Someone had allowed the Waste to grow. Someone who knew what they were doing. Iron banished a spirit to its haunted item, but the Waste was made of many spirits. It left and returned, each part, again and again. The damage did not stop the progress. Iron would never wholly banish it. And now, not even lead could hold it in.

"Who set it free?"

"It doesn't matter," the ghost said. "We were hidden. We were safe. And then you led it to us. You brought death to the dead."

"The Waste feeds on the living as much as the dead, bud. Whoever let it out has it in for everyone, and you're still whining about losing your spot in the tunnel rat society? If I destroy it, all of you little moles get to go back to your holes. If I don't, we're all in the same boat. You keep that in mind."

The ghost laughed, half-coughing, and tried to tear at Shane's wrist by digging bony fingers into his flesh.

"Good. You'll die. You'll know suffering when it rips your soul from your body, and you become another screaming mouth in the Waste's bulk."

The ghost struggled and writhed to break itself free. It did not care about saving itself, or the logic in helping Shane. It just wanted him and the others to suffer as it would.

"I'll spare you that fate," Shane said.

He pushed his weight down, and the ghost's neck crunched. Its body went limp, and its clawlike hands fell away from his wrist. Shane pulled, tearing the head from the neck and releasing a blast of energy that pushed him backward and shook the structure of the illusion.

Rain pelted him in the face again, and the other spirits were thrust back. He was on the hilltop alongside the others.

Coulson was grappling with two ghosts to keep Ventura safe. The spirits that had been in the illusion with Shane were regrouping. They circled like coyotes looking for an opening. Shane's patience had run out.

He ran to Coulson, taking the spirit of a man with great, leaking boils down his back and dragging him to the ground from behind. The ghost tried to speak but could get no words out as Shane jerked his head roughly to one side, breaking his neck.

The ghost's head cracked as Shane put pressure on it, locking eyes with Ventura and giving the man a quick nod to make sure he was doing well. Ventura returned the gesture as the ghost's skull buckled.

Another blast of energy buffeted against Shane, but he held fast and was on his feet again, taking aim at the closest spirit, breaking the ghost's wrist quickly and taking it to the ground with a kick to the back of its knee.

The number of spirits dwindled quickly. Coulson destroyed his foe a beat after Shane eliminated his. The ghosts of the hills were no fighters, and they provided little challenge. But they were at least observant enough to realize they had bit off more than they could chew, and that none would survive if they kept up the fight.

Shane stood, breathing heavily, soaked from head to toe. He looked across the hilltop and saw eyes watching from shadows, cracks, and crevices. None came forward. None spoke.

The failures swayed listlessly, and Coulson straightened his overcoat while Ventura got to his feet, wiping blood from a wound on his head.

"Stay hidden," Shane spoke to any ghosts close enough to listen, "or regret it."

He turned his back on the eyes that watched him and started walking again. The failures joined him a step behind, and Coulson gave Ventura a quick slap on the shoulder to get him moving as well.

He could not see Lab Four, even from atop the hill, but they were getting closer. The day was losing light, and the already dark sky was darkening behind the rain clouds. Soon, there would only be the lightning to guide them, and Shane did not look forward to navigating the flooded desert at night.

"Stay hidden or regret it," Coulson said quietly, mimicking Shane's voice. He laughed softly. "Solid line."

Before Shane could reply, a crackle of static cut him off. The radio he had taken from the Humvee hissed in his pocket, soft and muffled.

A voice that he could not make out said something, and Shane pulled out the radio, standing still on the hilltop to listen. He turned the volume knob all the way up and held the speaker to his ear as Coulson and Ventura huddled in, the failures shifting and swaying as they waited nearby.

The static broke, and the radio went silent for a moment.

"You out there, Ryan? Over."

Shane recognized Hawke's voice. He wondered if the man was somehow tracking the radio but didn't think it was a complicated enough piece of equipment to have that functionality. It was more likely that Hawke saw that Shane had taken the radio from the Humvee and guessed he'd kept it to listen in on them.

"Ryan, you still alive, over?"

"Sounds like we both are," Shane said.

He had wondered if the man had survived the Waste outside Lab Four. Now, they knew.

"Good to hear your voice," Hawke said. The radio went silent for a beat. "Just wanted to thank you for the run. It's been fun. Good luck."

The radio went dead.

# CHAPTER 13
## PLAN B

Shane stared at Ventura. The rain was letting up at long last but still fell in thin droplets at a brisk pace, enough to leave both men dripping from their noses and brows. The static on the radio remained steady and unbroken.

The range was limited, which meant that Hawke was probably within a few miles. He knew that of Hawke, and Hawke knew that of him, but the soldier was playing a different game now.

"That mean you're giving up and leaving town?" Shane asked.

There was a long silence. Shane did not want to stay still for long. The ghosts of the hill might launch a second attack, and if Hawke was tracking him, Shane didn't want to be so exposed.

They started off again, traversing the rocks and puddles on their way east, leaving what they had just encountered behind them.

"No," Hawke said finally.

Shane doubted the soldier was idly sending messages. He was doing something, keeping busy, and taking breaks to keep Shane engaged. There was no sound beyond the rain, not the rumble of engines or the whirring of helicopter blades. No one was close to them. Or at least not close enough to give themselves away.

"You think I'm going away?" Shane said to keep the man engaged. He heard faint sounds in the background. The other soldiers were talking, and something was happening, but the radio's sound quality was not sharp enough for him to pick up much.

"Soon enough. Sincerely—I mean this—you made things interesting, and I appreciate it. This post has alternated between years of mind-numbing boredom and these past couple of weeks of abject terror. We're all going to die out here, Ryan. We're all screwed. But you gave me a run for a day. Thank you."

It was not what Shane had expected, and it took him by surprise. He glanced at Ventura again, and the FBI agent widened his eyes and shrugged.

"Midlife crisis?" he suggested.

It was more than that, of course. Hawke seemed pragmatic and grounded, even if he was actively working to kill them and cover up the atrocities. Too pragmatic, from the sounds of things. He was resigned to losing.

"It doesn't have to be like this, Hawke. Help us take on the Waste. It can be destroyed."

Coulson shook his head as the static returned to the radio.

"You can't trust him," the ghost said. "He's not going to abandon his code to join the A-Team here."

"I don't need to trust him," Shane said. "I just need to use him, his men, and whatever tools they have to handle the dead. They have ghost guards locked in trunks on Humvees, and someone built that vault. Someone here knows how to handle spirits."

"That's what Dr. Bauman said. You never met Bauman. If you see the Waste again, look for a face near the left arm. Older guy with green eyes and very thin lips. That was him," Hawke said over the radio.

"You have files on me," Shane said. "You know enough of my past. You ever wonder how I survived all of that? This is what I do, Hawke. I'm the thing the ghosts worry about when they hear a sound in the dark. I'm what comes to take forever away from them, and I will end the Waste. *We* can end it."

The static hissed, and they began their descent down the far side of the rocky hills, back to the desert with its muddy dunes and secret pools. None of the ghosts tried to attack them again, or even follow them as far as Shane could see. They had given up, just like Hawke was doing.

Their trip down ended at the open mouth of a new mineshaft. More modern than those in the other mountain, the entrance was framed by thick timbers, and the tracks for mining cars came up to a stop a couple of yards from the entrance.

The tunnel pulled the air toward it, creating a draft and a faint moaning sound. The depths of the mine were hidden in darkness, but Shane didn't doubt the ghosts from above had retreated there and were still watching.

"That's good," Hawke said as Shane peered into the mine, his voice breaking the staticky emptiness. Then, he laughed. The signal was getting worse, crackling more as he spoke. "The thing the ghosts are afraid of. You've got this whole thing down, huh?"

"I'm serious, Hawke. We can fight it together."

"No, Ryan, we can't."

The signal degraded further, and Hawke's voice faded in and out. Either the weather was interfering, or they were getting farther apart.

"More people will die; you know that."

"No," Hawke said. "No one died here. There was never anyone in the desert. No one will ever hear about this. Good luck, Marine."

The static droned on.

"Hawke."

The rain was down to just a drizzle now as the blackness of the night sky consumed the desert and there was nothing to see in any direction. Shane started walking again, turning his back on the mineshaft. Coulson and Ventura stayed at his side, listening silently as they walked while the failures kept pace without making a sound.

"Hawke," Shane said again, louder.

No reply came over the radio. They walked for another minute, then two, and finally, he turned the knob and shut off the radio.

"What the hell did that mean?" Ventura asked.

Shane had no answer. Hawke had something planned, and it sounded extreme. He hadn't needed to talk to Shane. Maybe he had been sincere with his message. It wouldn't be the strangest part of their trip, but it was still perplexing.

Either Hawke and his men were leaving, or they were going to do something that would ensure no one survived. Was Hawke the sort of man to sacrifice his life in the line of duty?

Shane didn't know him that well, certainly not well enough to make such a judgment on his character. But he had made the same decision earlier when talking with Coulson and Ventura. They planned to take on the Waste knowing full well their odds of survival were virtually non-existent. Why should Hawke be any different? He had to give the man the benefit of the doubt. He would go to extremes.

As if hearing his thoughts, a light sparked to life on the horizon. It was swift-moving and traveled in an arc through the air above them. More joined. Shane counted a dozen and then a second volley, all coming from the southeast.

"Get down," he said loudly, dragging Ventura to the ground in a muddy lagoon. Both men splashed into the murky body of water, plunging below the surface.

Missiles sailed overhead, spreading like fingers on an opening hand. They screamed through the night sky and rained down to the west, peppering the earth with a series of booming explosions that lit the horizon so brightly that Shane saw the blast from under the water before he rose from it.

"The bunkers," Coulson said.

The ghost hadn't bothered to duck; he didn't need to. More bombs hit, larger explosions in a straight line directly west of them. A brutal wind whipped at them, spraying debris and a charred smell.

Shane lifted his head, still mostly submerged, as the brutal gust of the blast roared past them, creating waves in the pool.

"And the labs," Shane added.

Hawke had rained fire on everything. Any sign of the PULSE experiments, the Burners, and what had been done in the desert was destroyed in a series of earth-shaking blasts.

"Jesus. Tell me those aren't nuclear." Ventura was immersed to his chest in water.

Fire raged across the desert. Despite the sand and water and a lack of anything else, the missiles scorched the desert and burned with ferocity. Huge plumes of white smoke rose into the sky above where the missiles had detonated.

They were not nuclear. Shane recognized the smoke and the incendiary effects. Hawke had launched thermite bombs. If they had been closer to the targets, the smoke alone would have killed them.

Thermite burned up to five thousand degrees, as hot as the surface of the sun. It would burn through the bunkers, concrete, sand, everything. Nothing would be left but a seared hole in the world. Its only purpose as a weapon was to erase.

"You can't burn the Waste away, Hawke. You have to know that." Shane tried the radio again.

No reply came from the soldier over the radio. Instead, a second volley of missiles was launched from the base, curving through the sky into the near distance to the west. They were not targeted toward the bunkers this time, but Lab Three.

The ground shook violently, and the blinding white light of the thermite ignition turned night into day. The failures groaned and shimmered, sparking to life with their light briefly in response as though the explosions had called out to them.

Four bombs hit in the second volley, each one at the Lab Three site. Hawke was aiming not for the lab but at what was underground.

"He's trying to melt the nest." Coulson stood and watched with no fear of blindness.

The ground continued to rumble, and smoke billowed in great plumes that would have been visible for miles during the day. But at night, in the storm, they might have been invisible as deep in the desert as they were.

Shane stood as the glow diminished, looking back the way they had come. Hawke's plan had potential. If the thermite penetrated deep enough, if they had targeted the right spot, it was more than capable of melting bone down to nothing. The Waste's nest and the mass of haunted bones within would be destroyed. But it was not the Waste's only nest.

"Hawke, listen to me." Shane lifted the radio to his mouth.

No static answered as he pressed the key. He tried to switch channels and adjust the volume, but nothing happened. The water had shorted the device out. Their communication lines were closed. And Hawke had no idea the Waste was not based solely in the nest. He was going to succeed in making it angry and little else.

The rumbling grew stronger instead of diminishing as the blazing thermite grew dimmer as it sank deeper into the earth. It was not the explosions they felt anymore. Something else was shaking the ground.

"He called it back." Shane was annoyed by Hawke's lack of foresight.

The Waste was coming back. It possessed enough faculties to understand someone was attacking it and putting the bulk of its haunted items at risk.

It would be foolish to think of the ghost like other ghosts or even wholly like an animal, but it was no longer like any human spirit Shane had dealt with. And if it was more primitive and bestial in nature, it would react violently to someone threatening its home.

To the southeast, a new sound filled the night. Not missile launches; the attack seemed to be over now. Instead, there was a heavy thrum of helicopter blades as two choppers took to the air. Shane just barely made out the lights as they rose over the canyon base.

Shane cursed and helped haul Ventura out of the lagoon.

"Back to the mine." He looked from the agent to Coulson.

Both nodded, and they moved as a unit, trailing the failures to the mineshaft that stood shrouded in shadow a few dozen yards away. The ghosts would be waiting, and they would be underground on the Waste's turf, but they could not stay out on the surface with Hawke back on patrol. The soldier had made his endgame move.

Someone would have to die.

CHAPTER 14
# THE MAN IN CHARGE

Fire fell from the sky. The helicopters strafed the landscape, separating, and raining bombs across the desert. Explosions blossomed in great plumes again and again and again.

Shane ran, half dragging Ventura with his injured leg, while the three ghosts followed behind toward the waiting shaft. Darkness gave them cover, and it was unlikely the pilots had seen them, but Shane didn't want to bet on it.

They reached the mine entrance and barreled into the unknown, racing into the shadows and depths that waited behind. The way was slick, but littered with rubble and bolstered by the train car tracks to give them more solid footing. It was only a couple of yards past the entrance when Shane lost the ability to see anything.

He kept moving, taking the lead with a hand on the wall, while the others followed single file. Coulson could have done his light trick, but they would stand out like a spotlight for the choppers if he did it so close to the exit. They needed the darkness.

The ground continued to shake, part of it the nearby burrowing of the Waste, but the bulk of it the repetitive explosions from the helicopters as they destroyed everything in their paths. They were getting closer.

Shane had no sense of direction when it came to the Waste, where the ghost was coming from, or how deep it might have been. It had to be heading to the nest, or that was the most logical path that it was on, which meant it could get close to them if it hadn't already passed.

The helicopters were the greater threat. The Waste was occupied, at least for a moment. It was not hunting them. But the helicopters were approaching at speed. They needed to get deeper into the earth.

From the mouth of the mine, the thunder of the blasts grew louder. One of the helicopters was on an intercept course with the hills.

"Light it up." Shane looked back in the darkness.

Coulson's body came to life, a soft blue glow encompassing him head to toe instead of just around his hand as usual. He pushed past Ventura and silently took the lead.

They moved faster with the ghost lighting the way. This mine was cleaner and sturdier than the previous mine, with cleaner-cut walls and better support. Shane followed at Coulson's heels, most of his focus on watching his footing due to the water which ran in a shallow stream from the entrance.

They headed down into the ground, but the gradient was not as sharp as Shane had hoped.

The desert rumbled at their backs, and a flash of orange fire reflected along the damp walls. The stone over their heads shook and rumbled. The sound built, and when it seemed as impossibly loud as it could get, the next blast was somehow even louder.

Dust and stones rumbled and fell from the ceiling above them. The helicopter was strafing the hill, burning a path from east to west.

Ventura stumbled when a head-sized rock fell on him, scraping the burn wound open from his shoulder to mid-back. He screamed as he fell to his knees, and his back leaked blood and clear fluid as his body shuddered in pain.

The tunnel was an apocalypse of noise and rubble. Stones dislodged, but the support timbers held the bulk of it back. The sound drowned out everything. Shane couldn't even hear the cries of pain as Ventura steadied himself. His ears rang, and the rage of the thundering earth was all that filled his head.

Fire raced down the tunnel from outside like a living thing following their tracks. They had traveled as deep as they could in the time they had to escape, but the mine worked as a funnel, channeling the fuel and combustion reaction like a bullet down the barrel of a gun.

Flames licked and rolled against the wet walls of the mine and snaked toward them. Shane pulled Ventura, forcing him to scramble on all fours as he gained his footing. He ran as fast as he could, outrunning the blast by mere feet as the fire struggled and dissipated, lacking the fuel and power to continue onward.

The tunnel entrance had collapsed. The blast was cut off, but so were they.

A rush of hot air licked at their backs and made Ventura cry out again as heat ravaged his burn. It was hard to breathe for a moment. The oxygen in the tunnel was eaten by the brief flash of devastation. It took a few moments for the air to return, and for them to fill their lungs again, but for an instant, it felt like drowning in open air.

Ventura slumped to the floor and Shane stopped, leaning against the wall and breathing deeply. The FBI agent gasped and groaned, trying to get to his knees, and then giving up as he lay face-down on the tracks with water pooling around him.

For all the noise and sense of dread, the bombing run was quick. The attack choppers moved on, laying waste to more targets and destroying the surface world. The bombs were not thermite this time. This round was meant to burn and break whatever walked the sands. They were for Shane and Ventura.

The rumbling moved on, steady and unwavering. Shane wondered how many munitions the helicopters had packed, if they'd need to return to base for a restock, or if they had calculated where Shane must have been based on his radio signal and used just enough to scour that part of the desert.

"Oh, my God," Ventura groaned, shakily getting to his knees. "It feels like someone beat my back with a burning log."

"It looks like hell, if that helps," Coulson told him.

The ghost wasn't wrong. The burn across Ventura's back was shoulder to shoulder, from the back of his neck down maybe ten inches. The flesh was burned deep, second- and maybe third-degree burns damaged more by the rock that tore more skin away. Combined with running through the rain for hours and the water saturating the loose, burned flesh, the wound looked like nothing Shane had ever seen. It was a puffy red and yellow and white mess of blistered, puckered, torn flesh that wept blood and other fluids.

Ventura would only last so long with an untreated wound like that. The pain alone had to be horrible, but his risk of infection was almost certain. He needed to be treated and needed time to heal. Shane could not offer him either of those things.

"You have to leave me here." Ventura tried to sit up.

His arms shook like he was on the last of a hundred push-ups. He collapsed again. Shane crouched at his side, inspecting the wound on his back more closely.

"Leave you here? We're just getting to the best part. You're not crapping out now," he said.

Ventura breathed out into the streams under him, sputtering water as he scoffed.

"I crapped out a while ago. Adrenaline had me going this far, but I think that rock knocked it all out of me. I can't keep going, Ryan."

"You can," Shane said. "Because you don't want to die in this goddamn desert."

"I don't want to die in this goddamn desert," Ventura agreed. "But I don't think I have a choice. My leg is shot. My back… you don't have to tell me; I can feel it. I don't even know if I'd survive if we walked out free and clear right now."

Shane felt the urge to poke the man in the wound, to give him a jolt of pain as a motivator, but decided against it. Ventura wasn't used to that sort of motivation. He wasn't raised in that world. But Shane needed him to get his head in it, pain or no pain.

"You've been going all day. You've got a night left in you. If we're going to get killed by the Waste anyway, you need to be there," Shane said.

"Geez," the agent laughed. "You suck at motivational speeches."

"You do, Ryan," Coulson agreed. "Horrible."

Ventura rolled to his side, wincing as his back ground into rocks and the left cart track. He was breathing heavily, but the move at least allowed him to look at Shane.

"You guys go. It was always going to be you, anyway. I don't even have my iron baton to swing."

Pebbles broke free of the ceiling and clattered around them as the world continued to shake from dropping bombs and the raging Waste. Shane took Ventura on either side of the collar and forced him into a sitting position despite his painful protests. They sat, eye to eye, and Shane held him steady.

"Listen to me. I can count all my friends who are still alive on one hand. Most of the ones I lost, I had no chance of helping. But I'm not going to leave you in an abandoned mine outside of Las Vegas and let a staph infection kill you in another two days."

Ventura smiled, his face flushed red. He was soaked from the rain, but the moisture beading on his forehead was more sweat than water.

"Hey, don't be so cynical. I bet the ghosts will kill me long before an infection does."

Coulson sighed heavily and crouched with them.

"I can't deal with this manly melodrama anymore. You don't want to die, he doesn't want you to die, I don't want you to die, and the great circle of friendship is formed. Let me in again. Let me take over until we're done here."

"Take over me?" Ventura said.

"No, take over Venezuela. Yes, take over your body. I'm not going to feel that pain, and you won't have to. It'll be like… a really weird piggyback. If it doesn't work out, you'll die anyway. At least this way, you get a fighting chance," Coulson said.

Ventura sighed. Shane was doing a lot of work to keep the man upright because his body had essentially stopped trying.

"Sure. Okay."

"Alright, same as before," Coulson said. "Just this time I'm going to have to be a little more intrusive, keep your mind away from your body."

"I'm still going to be in here, right?" Ventura asked.

"Yeah, but more of a backseat-driver situation. It'll be weird at first, but you'll be fine."

"I trust you, Coulson," Ventura said. He turned to face Shane then and put a hand on the other man's shoulder. "I trust both of you."

"Circle of friendship." Coulson nodded. "Very touching."

The blue light winked from existence as Coulson's form fell into Ventura's, the two of them oozing together until darkness covered everything. Shane felt Ventura's hand slip from his shoulder, but he was still holding the other man by his shirt front.

Ventura shifted, his body shuddered, and then he pulled away. Shane let him go, standing in the dark and waiting to see what came next. The other man didn't make a sound for a long moment and then, slowly, a light grew in the dark of the tunnel.

It was not a full-body glow, it was just one hand like the torch lights Coulson had made before. Only it was not Coulson now, it was Ventura. His hand glowed a soft blue, and he lifted his arm until the glowing hand was next to his face.

"How do I look?" Coulson's words came out of Ventura's mouth.

"Like a half-dead guy," Shane said.

"Perfect. Feels like it's working okay. Now we just have to find a way out of here."

He turned to look at the failures, both spirits shifting and swaying, their burned bodies moving to their unknown rhythm.

"Hey. Can one of you guys manage a soft light? Guide the way through here?" Ventura asked.

The nearest of the ghosts sparked and flashed like a fluorescent light struggling to come on and then finally it stopped, settling on something notably brighter and whiter than Ventura's hand.

"Good enough," Ventura said. "Lead the way, get us out of here."

The ghost said nothing, but it began to walk, setting a quick pace as it navigated through the tunnel into the unknown.

# CHAPTER 15
# ENEMY MINE

The rumbling had nearly died down. The ground vibrated beneath Shane's feet, and it reminded him of walking in a city near subway tunnels. It was there, faint but perceptible and impossible to escape or fully ignore.

The bombs had stopped, or the helicopters had at least gone far enough from the mine that nothing they did resonated. The quaking that remained was the Waste. It was endless but not close. It droned on, and Shane wondered what the ghost was doing. The Waste was not something that could be forgotten.

Any other time they had perceived the sensation of the burrowing spirit, it was coming or going. It was traveling somewhere, and the rumbling that gave it away only lasted for so long. For it to continue at such a long stretch raised questions for which he had no answers. All he knew for sure was that it was hard at work.

Hawke's attack had provoked a response. It could have been saving its nest if it got there in time, transporting the mass grave to someplace new. It could have been doing anything. It did not think like a man, even a madman. It was virtually alien.

Something was unsettling about a mystery like the Waste. To know what was causing the earth to move, and how it was doing it, but to have no idea why, was more unnerving than having no answers. A partial mystery begged to be solved; a full mystery could at least be pushed to one side and ignored for the lack of context and information.

It was enough to know that the Waste had set about some monumental task that required extensive tunneling but not traveling. It worried Shane. But there was at least a degree of relief in the fact that it was far removed. Out of sight and out of mind was not always practical, but in the case of a seemingly indestructible burrowing spirit, it was better than nothing.

The deeper into the tunnel they went, the more rubble appeared in the path ahead of them. Shane would have expected the opposite, but it soon became clear that the destruction was not caused from above but below.

Much like the one they had traversed previously, the mine here had fallen victim to the Waste. It had not torn through it explicitly, but it had tunneled too close. The mines were hewn from rock, but they could still be very fragile. A tunnel burrowed below one, pulled apart by the savage hands of an unhinged spirit, was chaotic and unpredictable. The mine had suffered as a result. And the spirits they had encountered atop the hill, were set on edge at the same time. They feared the Waste the way the living feared them. The desert had birthed layers of horror.

At a branch in the tunnels, the left passage went down at an angle for only a short distance before the ground bottomed out. The mine was swallowed into one of the tunnels created by the Waste. Large piles of rock lay below them, partially filling the irregular, round tunnel that the spirit had burrowed through.

It followed the same path as the mine above it, at least from what Shane saw, traveling roughly east to west. They needed to head east, but traveling in a Waste tunnel was not ideal. He had no idea if Hawke had mapped any of them or was setting traps. Nor did he have any way to know if the Waste would be active in following its own footsteps. It was best to stay as out of sight as possible and off the radar in every way.

The passage continued at less of an angle, and the Waste had not tunneled under it, so it had never collapsed. They chose it as the only viable option and started to follow it.

In the glow of the failure's bright white light, Shane finally saw the spirits who had attacked them on the hill. They had barely entered the tunnel, perhaps traveling a dozen yards at most, when they appeared at the edges of the failure's light.

As before, the dead congregated, seemingly more confident and defiant, watching from behind the support timbers or around piles of small, fallen rocks.

Shane and Ventura stopped, and the failures stopped with them. There were two options, neither appealing in any way that mattered. Shane wanted a quick exit, and a way back to Lab Four. Instead, he would have to choose between one enemy and another. To press forward and fight the dead, or to backtrack and follow what the Waste had left.

"We're just passing through," Shane said. "Stay out of our way, and we stay out of yours."

"You are already in our way."

He could not see which ghost had spoken the words, but Shane didn't care which one it had been. The sentiment was likely true for all of them. They had been scared away on top of the hill, but there was nowhere else for them to go now. They were backed into a corner, and they would not be scared off again. If pushed, it would likely be their last stand.

"We don't have the time for this," Shane said.

A spirit crept over one of the rocks, dragging torn bits of flesh behind it, peeled away from its body like someone had removed strips before the man it once was died. The ghost's insides only partially filled that description. His guts had been pulled loose but not fully extricated. Pulpy, bloody masses of intestines and bloated organs dragged across the ground beneath him.

His face was just as ragged as the rest of him, his skin scraped away roughly like he had skidded down the rock and grated it off. Most of the front of the spirit from his thighs to his nose had been torn away in a horrendous accident that didn't bite deep enough to split him open. But his eyes remained, clear and piercing, and they stared into Shane's.

"You will have forever," the ghost said.

They came forward in a rush, a surge of limbs and ghastly, disfigured faces. They crawled across the floor of the mine, along the walls, and suspended from the ceiling like an army of man-sized locusts.

Shane cursed, backing away as the ghosts barreled forward. There were too many to fight at once, even with Coulson controlling Ventura's body. They were not fighters, but in terms of numbers, they would overcome the two men handily.

"Other tunnel." Shane pushed both failures by the shoulders to force them into motion. The two ghosts made no sound, following the instructions and rushing ahead, back to the caved-in floor that led down into the Waste's domain.

The rumbling shook the mine, and the Waste was still somewhere far off. Even if it came back, it seemed more focused on creating new tunnels than following old ones, accommodating its greater bulk and whatever whims drove it forward.

Ventura was ahead of Shane, ushering the failures to the hole. He didn't hesitate before pushing them over the edge and jumping down after them as they reached the fractured rock ledge that loomed over the hand-dug tunnel below.

Shane paused at the edge, choosing a landing site that would be less likely to result in a broken leg. He didn't have the benefit of preternatural reflexes the way Ventura now did and was not going to kill himself in an attempt to escape death.

The ghost with the shredded face was on top of him before he could descend. As Shane readied to drop to the nearest rock face—a flat segment of the collapsed tunnel that looked like it would hold his weight—the ghost leaped on him, dragging him to the ground and sinking icy teeth into his shoulder.

Shane cried out in pain and clutched at the ghost's head. The others were coming, the rush of dozens of spirits was mere feet away, and there was no time to remove the ghost or finesse any kind of escape. Instead, Shane rolled off the edge of the jagged rocks and fell below.

The distance between the mine shaft and the tunnel floor was not excessive. It was one of the Waste's older tunnels, and Shane suspected the drop was nine feet at best. He fell straight, gritting his teeth as the ghost gnawed on the flesh of his shoulder, and kept the spirit between himself and the ground. The spongy, not-quite-natural bulk of its body broke their fall against the edge of a rock, and the ghost's jaws released so that it could scream as bones snapped in its back.

Shane rolled awkwardly off the spirit, rattled by the fall but not nearly as injured as he could have been. The others huddled around the broken ledge above them. None dared to come down. The threat of the Waste was too great a fear to overcome.

"Help… me…" the ghost gasped, staring up at its companions. He was unable to move; the fall had fractured his spine.

"Should have listened." Shane stood over the spirit.

"You're still… going… to die here." The ghost grinned a gruesome smile that tore at his already shredded lips and exposed broken teeth.

Shane grunted. Ventura waited with the failures, the bright light illuminating the path that led back in the direction they had come, toward Lab Four. The thrum of the Waste's tunneling still vibrated, safely away from them at some unknown location. For now, anyway.

He felt the blood trickling down his chest under his shirt, flowing in a thin, sticky trail from the bite wound on his shoulder. The wound was deep, but he knew it was clean. A ghost's mouth did not spread infection.

Shane stood over the ghost. Above them, the others watched in silence. None came down. They all could have descended, killed Shane, and fled to safety in seconds. But they refused to enter the Waste's tunnel.

"Finish me," the crippled ghost demanded, a cruel finality in the raspiness of his voice. "But know that… even if I'm gone… you'll be… in the Waste… forever."

The ghost laughed then, a strained, dry chuckle. He glared at Shane and waited for him to drop to his knees, to take the ghost's ravaged face in his hands and crush his skull like he had done to the ghosts atop the hill when they fought before.

"When you're gone?" Shane said. "Where are you going?"

A silence passed between them, and the indignance in the ghost's expression faded to a slow understanding.

Shane turned his back and nodded to Ventura. They both started walking, and the failures led the way without prompting.

"Finish me!" the ghost shouted after him.

Shane said nothing. He did not even bother looking back at the broken thing in the rubble. There was no need.

"You can't leave me here! YOU CAN'T LEAVE ME HERE!"

His angry cries followed them through the Waste's tunnel until he gave in and begged his companions for help. Shane and Ventura were out of sight, following a soft curve to the southeast by the time the spirit's cries for help switched to desperate pleas for someone to come back for him. The others had left, and he was alone.

He would stay that way until the Waste returned. Or maybe forever.

CHAPTER 16
# ROLL THE DICE

The ghost had long since fallen out of earshot. Now, the only sounds were the distant pulse of the Waste and the footfalls of Shane and Ventura on the rocky tunnel floor.

There was no water in the tunnel. The rain had not filtered down, at least not into the segment they were walking on. It was the first time in hours they had been dry... or at least not getting wet. Their clothes were still saturated, and the tunnel was by no means warm enough to dry them with any great speed.

"We should go back to the base," Ventura said as they walked.

Shane raised an eyebrow. He had not considered it. There was nothing there for them unless they wanted to steal another Humvee that Hawke could shut down remotely.

"There are two choppers in the air right now, and we know they lost a pilot when the one chasing us went down. The base is probably undermanned right now. We can access their equipment, files, and communications. Anything that could help us is going to be there," he continued.

"This Ventura or Coulson talking?" Shane asked.

"Ventura, mostly. But the reasoning is sound," the other man said. "Whatever information they have about the Waste will be there. Weaknesses, maybe."

"If it had a weakness, they wouldn't be carpet-bombing the desert," Shane countered. "I'm not disagreeing that the base might have useful information for this thing archived somewhere; I just think it doesn't matter."

"How could it not matter?" Ventura asked.

"Because our timeframe is hours at most. You feel it out there digging. Whatever it's doing, it's going to finish sometime, and then what? It's coming for anything still living out here, or it's leaving. Both are going to end badly," Shane said.

"Maybe we can find something to keep it busy until Vincent gets here. Hawke might not have destroyed it, but you can't deny that he's got it distracted."

Shane sighed and stared at the other man. Ventura's eyes stared back at him, but Coulson was in there somewhere.

"No one's coming, Ventura," he said.

The other man scoffed.

"We just wasted all that time with Dezzy. He's going to find this guy; we just need to hold down the fort."

"We have hours," Shane repeated. "Hours. To live. Maybe. Unless it decides to ignore us and head to the next town, and then *those* people have hours. And the next town might have hours. Dezzy will be lucky to have found a phone by then."

"Jesus Christ, Ryan." Ventura stopped in his tracks. "What the hell are we doing, then? What difference does it make if we go to the base, or to Lab Four, or just wait here? What are we doing? What are *you* doing?"

He was angry, but Shane heard more in his voice. He knew all the answers to the questions he asked. Ventura was not naïve, he was just new to this, and there was a distance. He didn't want to accept that things could go so wrong so fast. He didn't want to face a loss.

"If you want to go to the base, I'm not stopping you," Shane said. "If you think that's where you need to be, you can go. Both of you. I'm heading to Lab Four."

"That's not much of an option," Ventura said. "Splitting up would be suicide."

"Lab Four was sealed for a reason. The only other thing they sealed out here was the Waste itself. Stands to reason that something powerful is waiting in there."

"And if it's just worse than the Waste?" Ventura countered. "Isn't that the most obvious reason? Another Waste? Something deadly and uncontrollable?"

"Maybe," Shane said. "I just don't think they would have created one monster, sealed it, and then done the same thing all over again. I think they did something else and couldn't keep control. All the labs made spirits that could be used as weapons. The power of the Burners hurts other spirits and hurts the Waste. I'm gambling on Lab Four being something too successful. Something that didn't want to follow orders."

"So, another Waste," Ventura repeated.

They weren't going to see eye to eye on the topic, and Shane had no interest in hashing it out. He knew that Lab Four was an extreme measure, but he was weighing all the options and could not come up with another solution. The wild card was all they had left.

If they avoided Lab Four, they would not succeed. In Shane's mind, it wasn't an if. The Waste was too powerful, and there was no way Dezzy would find Coulson's friend in time to make a difference. That was assuming their friend had the power to make a difference, another longshot.

He knew Ventura might be correct. Lab Four could have been home to nothing, to a complete failure, even to something worse than the Waste. But as it stood, the Waste was going to win. It would kill Hawke and his men. It would kill Shane and Ventura, and then, it would spread and grow stronger, and no one else would be able to fight it. It was the exact situation Hail Mary plays existed for. There was nothing else and, even if it failed, in Shane's opinion, it was better than nothing.

The failure lighting their way stopped abruptly, and the other one joined him. Shane was glad for a distraction from the conversation as he had no desire to keep repeating himself to Ventura. He'd made his intentions clear; it was up to the other man and Coulson to decide what they wanted to do.

They were no longer alone in the tunnel. A ghost stood in their path, several yards ahead, at the edge of the light produced by the failure. The spirit wore remnants of a uniform. It was not the desert camo that the soldiers working under Hawke wore, but the dark olive drab of an army service uniform.

The soldier was not waiting for them. It wasn't even looking in their direction. It stood motionless, staring at the wall of the tunnel. The drab trousers were melted to the ghost's flesh and stained with filth. Blood and char had replaced most of the original color. Half of the uniform jacket was burned away as well, along with the tie.

Shane saw several medals and some charred ribbons pinned to the jacket. The epaulets were missing, and Shane could not tell the soldier's rank. The profile view of the spirit's face showed glossy, almost white flesh that reflected the light of the failure as though it were coated in a thin layer of oil. No hair remained on the spirit's head, and all the features had been smoothed out. It looked to Shane like someone had been badly burned and then received skin grafts to temper the scarring, only the work had not gone well.

"That's a Burner," Ventura said, speaking Coulson's words.

Shane had not seen a Burner since before Hawke arrived. He was not sure any had survived the last attack by the Waste. This one looked better than the ones they had encountered at Bunker Eight. Most of its flesh was still intact, and it had yet to attack, which was an upside. But if it did, they had no place to go for cover.

There was no time to hesitate. Their experience with Burners had taught them that the spirits could be destroyed, but it had to be done before they had a chance to power up.

Shane broke into a run and, as though waking from a haze, the Burner lifted its head and turned toward him. He could see that the spirit had been a woman of slight build. Now, she was half burned away down the right side below the shoulder.

The Burner's light began to glow, and she locked dark, yellow-crusted eyes on Shane. He saw a flash of the name tag on her chest at the edge of the burned fabric, still saturated with blood and other fluids. Arkady.

Shane stopped as the light intensified, glowing brightly enough to conceal the Burner's face. Shane raised a hand, shielding his eyes.

"Arkady? Lieutenant Joanne Arkady?" he said.

The blinding light winked out. There was no gearing down; it just ended. Shane lowered his hand, and the ghost was there, nearly nose to nose with him, her smooth, burn-scarred face inches from his.

The dark eyes peered into his, and a faint aroma of burned meat clung in the air.

"Who are you?" she asked softly. There was no emotion in her voice, not anger or even anything that sounded curious.

"Shane Ryan," he answered. "We heard about you from someone named Eddie. In Lab Two."

The waxy flesh on Arkady's face wrinkled as she grimaced.

"Edward Walsh," she said. There was emotion in that name, something closer to disdain. "You work with him?"

"No. Had to rough him up a bit to get him to answer some questions," Shane said. "He mentioned you."

Arkady had traveled some distance from the lab. She was beyond the mile radius, which was curious, to say the least.

"Are you with the Phoenix Project?" the ghost asked. Shane shook his head. Eddie had mentioned that as well, but no one had explained it. Presumably, it was their code name, but that was nearly fifty years old by now.

"The project has been gone for a long time, as far as I can tell. Half a century. Thirty years, at least," Shane said.

"Thirty," Arkady said slowly, her eyes focused intently on Shane's. "Has it been that long? Seems like… weeks."

"Time can be hard to manage when you're dead," Shane said. He knew ghosts zoned out sometimes, and years passed in the blink of an eye.

"That's true," Ventura said, speaking Coulson's words. "Very easy to let time slip away when you never need to sleep, eat, or breathe."

Arkady narrowed her eyes at Ventura and then the failures. She was still uncomfortably close to Shane, emitting the funk of old meat that he could not grow used to no matter how much he smelled it.

"Who are you, Shane Ryan? And what are you doing down here?"

She must have recognized the failures. As part of the experiments, as a lieutenant who volunteered, she would have had some working knowledge of what was going on, even if the powers that be had kept a lot of the moving parts secret.

Lying to her would be a risk. Telling the truth would be just as risky. Sgt. Dylan had been unreceptive to Shane's plight and tried to kill him. It was possible Arkady, who had killed Eddie after the experiment that made her what she was, would be just as hostile.

Shane was still throwing Hail Marys. Whether it was Lab Four or Arkady, he needed to push forward and see what happened, even with the odds against him.

"We're going to Lab Four. We're going to destroy the Waste," he told the ghost.

"The Waste…"

Arkady spoke as though tasting the word. There were cobwebs there; something in her mind was not as sharp as it should have been. Standing alone in a Waste tunnel was indication enough that she was not all there anymore, but she was trying. She recognized the failures, and she remembered Eddie and the Waste. She was doing better than the Burnt Souls and Burners they had met so far. There was still a person there.

"They imprisoned it years ago," Shane said. "Trapped it near Lab

Three. But someone let it out, and it's gotten stronger. Bigger."

She looked at him with frustrated confusion. She was struggling to remember and understand. There were glimmers, moments when it seemed she grasped something. He knew so little himself that he could only give her a moment to sort it out and decide what to do.

"What…"

Arkady lifted her hands. Her right was a charred skeletal thing, black flesh clinging to black bone. The digits moved easily, controlled like living flesh, but they were long since burned to nothing. Her other hand was scarred and burned, puffy and blistered, and covered in gleaming, burned skin that was as smooth as wax.

"What happened to me?"

CHAPTER 17
# THE BURNER

The black bones of Arkady's hand flared with a white-hot intensity as she raked her fingernails down the wall of the tunnel. The stone melted away as if a hot knife was being pulled through butter. Globs of molten rock glowed red and oozed away as she dragged her fingers through it slowly and intentionally.

"I was part of the Phoenix Project." She was no longer facing Shane. "I volunteered... I think."

Her eyes searched for answers, as though Shane or Ventura or even the failures could guide her to the memories that she struggled to grasp hold of.

Shane did not understand the dynamics of what happened, the nature of the experiments, or how she was involved. But it was lost on her and only coming back now as she tried to put a voice to what she had endured.

He imagined how they structured such a program. Someone in the desert had inadvertently learned that radiation could affect the ghosts born from those deaths. Maybe something had been observed in Doomtown or a random test site when they set off one of their endless bombs.

The layers of secrecy behind such a project were impossible to fully imagine. In a world where few people knew ghosts even existed, setting up the program would have taken much careful planning that also happened at extremely high levels.

Even back in the fifties, people did not play with nuclear weapons without serious pull. The PULSE experiments, Project Phoenix, Doomtown, and the Waste were all the highest-level stuff Shane could imagine. There was a reason Hawke didn't wear a uniform that even identified his branch of the military.

"They were to use radiation. They said it would make us immune to the Russian weapons. We could fight through nuclear blasts and hit them at home if they tried to attack us."

It was a plausible lie at a time when the reality of what was being done—about the nature of the power involved—was hard for a layperson to understand. People knew the horrors of nuclear weapons, but they didn't fully understand how they worked or why they did what they did. This was the age of the atomic future. While they were scaremongering about weapons, they also were putting radioactive isotopes in drinks and calling them invigorating tonics. They were promising rocket ships to the moon and atomic robots. Why wouldn't someone believe powerful benefits could be gleaned from the safe and responsible application of that power?

"You didn't know what would happen?" Shane asked.

Eddie had said she was a volunteer. Doc had been adamant that the participants had volunteered and were even eager to give their lives to the project he worked on. It was not impossible. Shane knew soldiers who would rabidly support any plan they thought would give them a leg up on an enemy. Any procedure that would support our side and lay our enemies to waste. Not everyone would be so blind in following orders, but some would. There were always some.

He was not surprised to hear that the volunteers were misled. It was easy to get people to sign up for something if they didn't know all the details. Later, everyone could feel better about their involvement because, win or lose, no one was involved against their will. No one was forced. It made it all sound clean.

"I died," she said. Shane was not sure if she was answering his question. "I remember it… I remember that goddamn room…"

She turned to face not Shane but the failures that waited behind him.

Shane stepped out of her way as she walked to the one still glowing and reached for it, lifting its face with her hand, and looking into the empty sockets of the skull.

"This is what they did to you, too."

The failure's empty eyes were pointed in her direction, but there was only dead space there, shadow, and nothingness. The ghost's jaw parted slightly, and a sound like a tired sigh escaped.

Arkady covered her mouth with her hand and stepped away. She looked at Shane with panic in her eyes. Real emotion, raw and sudden, as memories and feelings came back.

The ghost touched her face with her good hand, the one still covered in enough flesh to feel something. She traced the smooth, waxy lines of her jaw, her missing lips, and the puffy, featureless flesh up to the top of her head.

Shane had rarely talked to Carl about returning from death. Eloise was not fond of the topic, either. It was a very personal thing, and it made sense. It was like a second birth, in a way. Becoming part of the world anew, in a vastly different way, must have been jarring in ways a living person could never fully understand.

Maybe that was why some ghosts lost much of their humanity in the transition. Maybe their minds couldn't handle crossing the bridge from life to death and accepting what they had become, especially with the physical changes that came with it. It could not have been easy to adjust or to even accept it.

"Am I a monster?" She looked at the failures.

Both were less than human in appearance. It was impossible to tell if either of them had even been male or female. Their identities had been stripped by the radioactive fires that had killed them and eaten them down to little more than bones and scraps.

Unlike Arkady or most spirits Shane had encountered, the failures were more like blank slates. They moved like automatons. Whatever Dezzy had done by speaking to them had reset them somehow, made them less aggressive and more obedient, and they were off and running as a result. They had no personality or spark of who they might have been. That was the true failure of their creation. The experiment had killed the individual in body and mind. Were they monsters, or something even less?

"No," Ventura answered before Shane could.

The FBI agent settled on the ground, leaning against the wall of the tunnel before Coulson rose from him, leaving the flesh of Ventura behind. The living man sighed, exhausted and in pain as the sensation of his wounds must have swept back in full force now that the ghost was gone.

Arkady stared at Coulson, and he approached her slowly.

"Look what they did to me," she said.

"I know," he replied.

Eddie had explained some of the process of making a Burner. Not just killing Arkady and making her into a spirit, but the process of torturing her once she was dead, prodding her in a room lined with iron rods, again and again, forcing her back to her haunted item over and over until she was forced to exert control over her powers just to stop it.

Coulson had been especially perturbed by Eddie's story. Shane imagined it was easier for him to appreciate both sides of the coin. Coulson fought ghosts but still could relate to them on some level. Arkady's story had struck a nerve.

"They mutilated me!"

"They did," Coulson confirmed. "They burned and tortured you. But you are free now."

He stood close to her, smiling in an aloof sort of way. She stared at him like he was an idiot.

"Free? To do what? I'm a goddamn monster!" She screamed, her hands flaring with white, searing light.

"Free to do anything," Coulson continued. "To stay here. To leave. To experience eternity however you like. To get revenge."

She balled her hands into fists, and the light muted. Shane looked away, keeping his eyes downcast as the two ghosts talked.

"I already killed Walsh," she said. "I got my revenge."

"Eddie was nobody," Coulson said. "He was doing what they told him to do. Just one cog in a much bigger machine. The people who made you also made the Waste. And it's loose now. It's consuming everything it can. And it will never stop."

"I remember it…" she said. "It was… they said there was an accident. Something overloaded. Something broke."

"And it killed a lot of people. Fused them together like melted wax. Gave birth to the Waste."

"No," Arkady said. "That came after. The deaths weren't accidental."

Coulson glanced at Shane. Arkady's anger was flaring again, and Coulson was trying to keep her calm and level.

"Dr. Shaw," the Burner said. "Dr. Shaw did this."

"Who is Dr. Shaw?" Shane asked.

"He ran Project Five. He made the Waste. He made all of us."

She turned her back on Coulson and Shane to face the wall of the tunnel, muttering under her breath. Rock dribbled from her hands where she leaned against it, and the air began to fill with steam as the dampness and heat mixed.

"They made it on purpose?" Coulson asked. "What purpose?"

"Weapons," Arkady said. "Always weapons. That's all it ever was. Not to protect anyone; to keep us safe. Just to kill."

"He must have thought it could be controlled," Ventura said. "They had to have thought that."

Shane agreed, but something was missing. A step in the plan had been overlooked or forgotten. Only a fool, after seeing how the failures and Burnt Souls failed to live up to expectations, would intentionally produce something like the Waste without a small, more controllable trial run.

Unless, of course, there *had* been smaller trial runs. Maybe that three-part ghost Shane had encountered in the cavern below the first mine was not a piece of the Waste; maybe it was a first run.

If they had been able to exert some level of control over smaller Wastes, someone could have been stupid enough to intentionally make the large one. But Shane still didn't understand how control was maintained. It was inhuman and lacked rationality. What had convinced anyone that it would listen to commands?

"Maybe," Shane said. "But why would they think that?"

No one had an answer, Arkady included. She was a volunteer with no access behind the curtain. What they did had been done to her, not with her.

"Is Shaw still alive?" Arkady asked.

"I have no idea," Coulson answered. "We're trying to stop the Waste; that's our only goal right now."

The light in Arkady's hands winked out, and only the glow of the failure remained, a relief compared to the soldier's blinding brightness.

"If you threaten his pet, you threaten him. They planned to make a cage for it, a place to trap it. He was furious. I remember him railing against the idea. Killing it will hurt Shaw."

She nodded and looked from Coulson to Shane.

"I will kill it. Let me kill it for you. That will bring him out. If Shaw is alive, that will draw him out."

The program had ended decades ago. Whoever Shaw was, Shane was almost positive he was no longer around. Even if Shaw was alive, he would not be out in the desert, puttering around a lab as a senior citizen.

Arkady was a Burner, though. She was rational, powerful, and out for revenge. Shane was not about to turn her down.

"Then let's go destroy a monster," he said.

CHAPTER 18
# THE NEST

Arkady walked with the failures. She had not tried to speak to them again after the first one couldn't answer her initial question. Shane didn't think anything was inside either of the spirits that could engage with her. Their minds had been taken from them almost completely. The way they stared at nothing, simply swaying in place when they stood still, Shane didn't think anything would be discovered in there. Nothing hidden waiting to be unleashed. They were hollow. It was like they had died a second time but kept going, the ghosts of ghosts.

Nonetheless, the lieutenant still recognized a connection between them. They had probably been fed the same story she had. They were told they would be heroes. When they were burned to their souls, they likely thought they did it for their country.

Coulson returned to Ventura's body. The FBI agent was not in as much pain as he had been, but he was exhausted, and the wounds on his back and leg were taking their physical toll, even while the ghost operated his body.

The spirit could keep Ventura going indefinitely. He probably could have kept Ventura going if he wasn't conscious. Maybe even if he was dead, Shane wasn't sure. But left to his devices, Ventura was too exhausted and weak.

After they finished what they were doing, destroyed the Waste, and escaped the desert, Ventura would need serious medical treatment. His back was festering with bacteria, and the infection could be life-threatening. Wallowing in desert lagoons had done him no favors.

With any luck, the FBI would at least take him back into the fold when he recovered. His assist in taking down Bennet Ross in Las Vegas had been mostly overlooked, but now, he could help them account for what happened to the town of Benton. That had to be worth something. All he had to do was survive.

The odds of defeating the Waste had never been good. Ventura's fears were well founded, but the situation was growing less grim. Or turning in their favor, at least. Enough that Shane believed they could do serious damage to the spirit even if they couldn't destroy it. Between him, Coulson, Arkady, and the failures—if they could be trusted to go off when they needed to—they could tear apart the ghost.

Shane hated having to rely on so many "ifs", but the addition of Arkady opened the door to more possibilities. If Lab Four paid off, they would have even more. There was hope, and that was better than a swift kick in the ass.

The shaking in the earth that had become so prevalent and expected stopped suddenly. Shane stopped as well, but the ghosts continued forward, none of them having the sensitivity to feel that the vibrations were no longer happening. Coulson must have been numbing Ventura's ability to feel anything to help him deal with the pain.

"The Waste is gone," Shane said.

Ventura looked him in the eye and raised an eyebrow.

"The quaking stopped," he added.

It had either left the desert or reached whatever goal it sought. Shane suspected the latter as the stop was so abrupt. It was not something that dwindled like it had fled the area.

"You can feel it in the rock?" Arkady asked from up ahead. She was still walking with the failures, pursuing their goal.

"Not anymore," Shane said.

"It seems to have passed this way at some point," she said.

Shane looked ahead to where the ghost stood. The failures continued

127

forward several steps, letting the white light reach further into the tunnel. Piles of rubble blocked their path forward where a second, larger tunnel bisected the first. The Waste had crossed over its own tunnel, heading northwest, and the path east was lost where the earth had caved in.

"You have to be kidding," Ventura said. Shane opted to curse and approach the piles of fractured stone. Access to the new tunnel was only partially blocked where some of the exterior walls and the roof had collapsed in the wake of the monstrosity, but the far side of the tunnel was obscured.

Shane climbed onto the rubble, looking for gaps or weak points. Everything was wedged firmly.

"Can you see if there's a way through?" he asked Arkady. He didn't want to risk digging a hole and collapsing with it, but a ghost could pass through easily.

"I don't go through things," she replied.

Shane looked at the ghost and cocked his head.

"What does that mean?"

"It means I do not go through things."

"It doesn't matter," Coulson said from within Ventura. "There's no way we can clear a safe path. It's too risky."

Shane climbed down from the rubble and stood in the center of the new tunnel. One branch returned almost in the direction they had already traveled. The other was aimed more toward Hawke's canyon base, assuming they were still heading as straight as Shane thought.

"Light Bulb, head over there for a sec," he said to the glowing failure, pointing down the southeast tunnel.

"What did you just call it?" Arkady asked, confused.

"We don't know his or her name," Shane answered.

"It's a clever nick name, if you ask me," Ventura added. Shane had no doubt it was Coulson who spoke.

The ghost did as instructed, walking down the tunnel with an unsteady gait. The passage curved within a few yards and then came to an abrupt stop. At first, Shane thought the Waste must have doubled back on itself but as the failure kept walking, he saw the shadows shifting along the floor.

Rather than ending, the passage took an abrupt turn straight down. The Waste had dug up from much deeper in the earth.

The failure walked right to the ledge and stopped, illuminating what was now a pit rather than a tunnel. Shane joined him, leaving the others behind at the junction, and looked into the darkness. It appeared bottomless from where they stood, a ten-foot-wide hole into the bowels of the world.

"How deep do you figure that is?" he asked Light Bulb.

The ghost moaned softly, and Shane used the top of his boot to kick a fist-sized rock over the ledge. The stone clattered off the walls and vanished. He waited, counting off the seconds in his head, but he never heard it hit bottom. He stopped counting at fifteen.

"Where does it go?" Ventura asked as Shane rejoined the others with Light Bulb in tow.

"Halfway to hell from what I see," he said. "This is our only option."

They would find a way out somewhere down the line. The Waste was surfacing and caving in mineshafts across the desert, so there would be a way out, but not where they wanted to go. Their only other choice was back to the mine and the ghosts waiting for them.

There was nothing to discuss; they had to act. Light Bulb lit the way and led them down the new, wider tunnel toward whatever waited. The cutting of the stone was smoother in this new passage, with the swaths gouged by the Waste's many hands more even. It was improving at what it did, growing stronger and faster based on the pattern in the rock. It was learning.

The Waste was still made of human intellect. There were many minds within it. Maybe they were lost to madness, drowning in a sea of screaming voices that shared a body, but it still must have had instinct. Intuition,

IAN FORTEY AND RON RIPLEY

observation, adaptation. Everything the living excelled at, and even single spirits, the Waste should have had in abundance. Just because it didn't know it was learning and adapting didn't mean it wasn't.

The longer the Waste was free, the more dangerous it would become. It would learn and become crafty and devious. Anyone left to fight it would surely underestimate it. Shane feared falling victim to that. Maybe it was wrong to think of it as mindless. He was not positive that was the case. No one could say for sure how intelligent the ghost was or how much humanity still sparked within it.

Shane tried not to focus too much on time as they walked, but it was impossible. The wasted minutes weighed on him. They had not heard the Waste in more than an hour. It could have made it to Las Vegas in that time. He hated being cut off, sealed away beneath the earth in a damp tunnel with no idea what was happening outside.

No one made conversation. Ventura was too exhausted, and Coulson was keeping him going. Arkady was not social, and it suited Shane fine. He liked the company of the failures. Ghosts that went where they were told to go and didn't complain or hesitate seemed like reliable companions. Not that he would have shared that with Carl or Eloise. Or Coulson, for that matter.

Light Bulb began to slow and caused its companion to do the same. Arkady slowed as well, and Shane was unsure of what the problem was for a moment. The tunnel ahead showed no roadblocks standing in their way. But as he passed the glowing failure, a sound reached his ears.

He stopped and raised his hand, making Ventura stop as well. No one moved. Somewhere ahead in the dark, metal hit metal. It sounded like hammering or something being torn apart. Nothing like the sounds of the Waste; this was smaller scale and much more subtle.

Shane stood still with his ear turned toward the darkness and closed his eyes, focusing on what he heard.

A voice echoed back. It was faint, far away, and too difficult to make out what was being said. But it was a person's voice, someone shouting at someone else. There were men underground with them.

"Where do you think we are right now?" Shane asked Ventura and Coulson, keeping his voice down so it would not travel to whoever waited ahead.

He was trying to keep a map straight in his head. It was difficult underground, with the winding of the tunnels and no sense of distance or direction. But he was tracking their pacing, keeping a rough idea of distance.

"Past the point where we came in from the tunnels," Ventura said.

"Back to Lab Three?" Shane asked. It couldn't be that far off. If the tunnel was curving a little more west than he thought, it was possible.

"The nest," Ventura said softly. The tunnel could have been one of the many paths back to the Waste's nest.

"Cut the lights," Shane told Light Bulb. The ghost complied without hesitation, its white glow clicking off as though a switch was flicked.

They proceeded in darkness and silence. The failures followed at the rear while Shane and Ventura took point. The sounds grew louder as the tunnel curved slightly left, and soon, the moisture on the walls began to reflect the yellow glow of lights ahead.

The voices became more distinct, not just a pair of individuals but many voices. At least a dozen. Men shouted orders and progress reports. As they rounded a final bend, the end of the tunnel came into view, and Shane ducked, getting the others to stop.

The nest waited for them ahead, the tunnel opening into the familiar cavern they had discovered a short time earlier. Only now, emergency lights were set up throughout the cavern and soldiers were busy working.

"Charge seven," someone yelled.

Shane watched as men in pairs wired charges around the vault. The bombing run had either destroyed what they expected it to or just distracted the Waste enough to keep it out of the way. Hawke and his men were now wiring the Waste's remains with more explosives, probably thermite charges, to eliminate the skeletons.

Other men were on shaky-looking scaffolds, setting up a shell around the vault. They had a pulley setup and were moving heavy metal plates into place. Lead, Shane assumed by the bulky look and the way they moved. They were making a shell, not to keep the Waste in, but to keep it away from the remains so they could melt them down in hopes of destroying it.

Their plan would fail. They were wasting manpower and time.

Worst of all, they were in Shane's way.

# CHAPTER 19

# FIRE DOWN BELOW

"Now what?" Ventura whispered at Shane's side. "You want to go in, guns blazing? Even though neither of us has a gun?"

Shane said nothing. He did not want to be stuck at the nest, and definitely not with a squad of Hawke's men or enough thermite to melt a hole to the center of the earth. They needed to hit Yuri's tunnel and get back up to Lab Three—if it was still intact—then cross the desert to Lab Four again. Sneaking past the soldiers was a possibility; they were focused on the vault more than the cavern around it, but getting through without being seen was not a simple prospect.

The failures could follow instructions, but Shane doubted their stealth. A decision had to be made quickly. The Waste could return at any moment, and once they set off a charge, it would feel the destruction of any of its haunted items and return immediately to protect what was left.

"We can make it to the tunnel," Shane whispered, nodding to the left.

There was an unobstructed path around the edge of the cavern with only a few stalagmites in the way. The nearest of Hawke's men were on the scaffold, at least ten yards from the entrance. With the lights pointed toward the vault, Shane and the others would be obscured by shadows and glare.

"Who are these men?" Arkady joined Shane and Ventura at the cavern entrance. She stood in full view despite the others having ducked for cover. Ghosts did not think about hiding.

"Company, east face!" someone in the cavern yelled.

Shane cursed as a rattle of rounds being chambered filled the space and a pair of lights were redirected to the tunnel.

"Don't let anyone set off those bombs," Shane yelled at the failures, running from the tunnel entrance into the cavern with Ventura at his side.

Soldiers opened fire, peppering the walls with bullets as the two living men ducked for cover below rock formations. Arkady's hand burst to life with blinding light, and a beam like a white laser cut across the space, slicing light poles in half and melting deep runnels into the lead walls of the vault.

Men ducked out of the way of the Burner's attack while the two failures followed her lead. Their less focused light flickered to life and went off in bursts, searing segments of rock as Hawke's men scrambled to avoid the blasts.

Shane could not see Hawke in the group, but the chaos had made it all but impossible to keep track of anyone in the blinding lights and irregular landscape. The failures had begun to strobe, blinding flashes and then darkness, again and again, making it impossible for anyone on either side to see what they were doing.

Arkady had destroyed most of the artificial lights, leaving only a few on the far side of the vault, and the faint glow of the Waste's remains as light source.

Gunfire went off randomly from multiple sources. Few rounds were being fired toward Shane; most of it seemed to be panic or suppressing fire as though to intimidate the ghosts.

Low to the ground, Shane took the lead ahead of Ventura toward the tunnel that led to Lab Three. He kept his eyes on the wall and away from the vault, limiting the effects of the failure's flashing as best he could.

Something collided with him when he was halfway to the exit. Arms like ice wrapped around him and squeezed, a brutal bear hug that was so powerful that it prevented him from drawing a breath.

The ghost of a massive man, nearly six inches taller than Shane with arms like a bodybuilder, had tackled him to the cavern floor. Hawke had brought more ghost guardians with him.

Shane had not seen the ghost coming and, trapped under its bulk, could not get a bead on it as it attacked him. The ghost rolled him over, crushing his rib cage as it locked its hands across his chest and arched its back, putting pressure on.

White lights flashed before Shane's eyes as he stared at the cavern's roof, pocked with shadow-filled tunnels dug by the Waste. Shane tensed his muscles, his arms pinned tightly against himself, and slammed his head back, banging his skull against the face of the huge ghost. Their height difference meant his head hit the spirit in the mouth. The pain in his head was worth it as he heard teeth crunching, breaking off in the ghost's jaw.

"Hey!"

The ghost's grip had not loosened after the attack, but a shout from Ventura distracted it enough that Shane was able to do it a second time. The back of his skull slammed into the ghost's face just as Ventura, guided by Coulson, kicked the spirit in the side of the head, nearly clipping Shane at the same time.

With a growl of anger, the big ghost released its arms. Shane slipped free and rolled onto his hands and knees, facing his attacker while staying out of the way of the stray bullets that blindly whipped across the cavern.

"I'm going to—" the ghost began, unable to finish his sentence before Ventura's foot crunched into his jaw from the side, breaking it.

Shane was on the ghost in an instant, putting enough pressure on his jaw to break it off, pulling it free in one hand while he used his other to force the ghost's head against the cavern floor.

Someone screamed across the room as a blast of Arkady's targeted fire split them in half. Shane's elbow came down hard on the ghost's temple, and the skull cracked. A second blow and it broke, destroying the spirit with a violent blast that hurled Shane against the nearest stalagmite.

The cavern was getting warmer, and Shane felt sweat trickling down his back. Every flash from the failures was like someone lighting a new fire, scorching the air around them. Arkady's fire, while more controlled, was far more intense. She was blasting toward anything that moved now, cutting soldiers down with no effort.

The failures had made their way to the vault. Hawke's remaining forces had taken cover behind the walls that still stood, and the two spirits were taking the fight to them.

A second ghost had circled to Shane and Ventura, less hasty than his recently departed companion. This one was smaller and thinner, but it had a crueler look in its eyes. Blood ran in a constant gush from the ghost's nose, and his hair hung loose and greasy about his shoulders. Bloodshot eyes regarded Shane and Ventura with caution.

"Why you getting in the way, hmm?" the ghost asked. "Why you fighting to protect this thing?"

"We're just passing through, buddy. Your guys fired the first shot," Ventura said.

The ghost grinned, and the deluge of blood from his nose curved over his lips and filled his mouth.

"Just passing through. Mmm, well. How 'bout that?"

The ghost crouched low and began to scuttle like an insect, circling toward Shane.

Another soldier screamed as a blast of blinding light filled the vault. The failures melted a segment of the wall, crushing two men under a splash of molten lead. Inside the vault, the liquid metal flowed onto the mass of fused skeletons, burning and coating the bones.

The ground began to shake, a soft rumble at first, but something distant that was growing closer. The Waste had felt the lead on the haunted remains. They had summoned it back to its nest.

"It's coming," Shane said to Ventura.

The bloody spirit took the momentary distraction as an opportunity to attack. Shane's jaw clenched, anger taking root deep in his gut. He had no time for this.

"Arkady, it's coming! Round them up!" he shouted at her as he met the bloody-faced spirit head-on. She either did not hear or did not care to listen. Shane had to return his attention to the bloody ghost. No finesse, and nothing fancy. It was time to kill.

He plunged his fingers into the ghost's eyes. Whatever the spirit had expected as an opening attack, it was not that. Shane's thumbs tore into cold, gelatinous flesh and plucked out a slurry of not-quite-real tissue that quickly faded from existence as he hurled the ghost to the cavern floor where Ventura crushed its head with a single stomp.

The blast of energy washed over Shane, and the rumbling in the cavern increased until fragments of rock began to fall from the ceiling.

"Guys, kill the lights," Shane shouted, getting to his feet.

The failures heard and listened, their blazing flashes stopping immediately as they both turned and wandered back to Shane, leaving the half-melted vault wall. A few of the surviving soldiers rose and took more shots until someone called for a ceasefire. Hawke was there, on the far side of the cavern, a rifle in hand and aimed at Shane.

"What the hell are you doing here, Ryan?" the man yelled.

"Trying not to die," Shane yelled back.

"You're not doing a good job."

"You could put down the gun."

"I could—"

Arkady's blast melted the end of the rifle before Hawke could finish his thought. The soldier cursed and threw the red-hot weapon to the ground. Shane was running with Ventura barely a step behind.

The failures were making their way slowly across the cavern when Arkady finally took notice of the others. She moved swiftly, sweeping at the vault with a beam of blinding light to distract the soldiers and force Hawke to take cover as the rumbling became almost deafening.

Rock fell in huge chunks from the southern wall of the cavern. A hole, the biggest Shane had seen, collapsed as a swarm of hands and arms punched through the stone, gripping the outside edges of the tunnel, and propelling the mass forward.

The light in the cavern was severely diminished, so what Shane saw come from the tunnel moving at a breakneck speed was wreathed in shadow. Fingers, hands, and arms by the dozen moved like a writhing mass of centipedes. They pulled the bulk of the Waste into the open, the pulsating torso mass made from human chests, abdomens, and heads bound together in a twisting flesh pillar.

The many faces shrieked as one as the tunnel birthed the Waste into the room, their eyes all locked on one thing: the vault.

"Light it up, now!"

The command came from Hawke, a decisive order bellowed in a loud voice to be heard over the fury of the Waste as it collapsed a series of older tunnels behind it.

Charges ignited across the lead panels that had been erected over the vault. Shane had thought they were building a new shell, but he was mistaken. He had misunderstood how they planned to make it work.

White hot metal illuminated the cavern and began to flow like water. Liquid lead splattered the remains of the Waste, and the fused skeletal remains of the spirit were washed with it as the vault began to melt, finishing the work that the failures had started.

The Waste moved like a twister, a non-living storm of bodies surging and writhing in a serpentine form that constantly reached and grasped at everything. The many voices howled as the lead drowned out the haunted bones that it had been keeping safe, searing flesh off the victims of Benton even as it entombed them.

Arkady's hands blazed to life, and Shane tried to tell her to stop. The cavern was shuddering, the latest tunnel from the Waste was still collapsing, and the arms were yanking at stalactites as it pulled itself toward its nest.

The Burner punched a hole through the Waste, the white light cutting clean through the larger spirit's torso but not slowing it down. It reached the vault and the pool of glowing metal as it concealed everything that had been there.

Buried in lead, any normal spirit would have been trapped forever. The Waste did not even slow. As Shane had guessed, it was not bound to just those remains.

The Waste shrieked as the last of its bodies were consumed. The many hands began digging, splashing the molten lead across the cavern, scorching Hawke's men while other hands caught those who ran and ripped them apart.

The flying lead splattered the walls, mixed with the incendiary chemicals of the bombs, and ate holes in the stone. None of it touched the Waste, but any of it could have killed Shane or Ventura.

"Go!" Shane yelled at the failures.

The tunnel to Lab Three had collapsed. But past it, across the cavern, Hawke fled into another tunnel.

Shane was steps behind.

# CHAPTER 20
# FOR YOUR LIFE

Screams pursued Shane down the tunnel. First, the screams of Hawke's men, and then, the manic, aimless rage-filled cries of the Waste. Arkady and Ventura kept pace while the failures had to be prodded but were not resistant to moving with speed if forced.

The smell of burning flesh floated hot and pungent with them, overwhelming the chemical smell of molten minerals and metal that would surely be deadly on its own. Sweat stung Shane's eyes as they moved blindly toward where Hawke was leading them.

He had no idea if the tunnel was how Hawke and his men had gained entry to the nest, or if the man was just fleeing in a panic. He would not know until they reached the end of the line, a gamble that could get them killed. But with the Waste scattering thermite and molten lead to the corners of the cavern, there was no alternative.

The tunnel curved around itself, winding back and forth in a haphazard fashion. Even with one of the failures lighting the way, it was impossible to catch sight of Hawke with the number of twists and turns that prevented them from seeing ahead.

The Waste screamed behind them, and there were words in the howls. Nothing that Shane could make out, but he was certain the multitudes were saying things. Maybe it was nonsense, the vented frustrations of the many parts. It was not worth waiting to make it out.

The earth shook, but Shane could not tell if the immense spirit was pursuing them or still salvaging its remains from the metal. The sounds of its enraged cries grew quieter the deeper they ran, though, and soon enough, there was only the rumbling of the earth, faint and intermittent as the monster tore at something in the cavern. It was not yet moving or pursuing, but that would not last.

The air in the tunnel became less heavy and less burned as they ran. Shane kept as hard a pace as he could, knowing their ghost companions would not mind and Coulson could push Ventura harder than he could have handled on his own. The younger man's body would pay for it when they separated, but it was better than being dead.

Shane was drenched in sweat, adding to the already clammy feeling of clothes soaked from hours in the rain. It felt like he was hauling a pack with an extra fifty pounds of gear by the time the air cleared enough to smell the desert again.

Soon enough, the tunnel floor glistened with runoff, filtering through cracks so it didn't pool too heavily in any one spot. The farther they went, the deeper the water became. Shane was sloshing up to his ankles by the time they reached the mouth of the tunnel, which opened onto what looked like a shallow river.

"It's the canyon," Ventura said as they spilled out into a narrow gap between rock faces not quite as wide as a city street.

Shane looked up, following the edge of the rock with his eyes. He couldn't say where they were, but a trio of Humvees were parked in the shallow water, now mostly drained since the rain had stopped. It was the same canyon where they had escaped Hawke and his men previously. They were near Lab Four again. And the base.

One of the Humvee engines cranked loudly, a repetitive whirring as it tried to turn over and start. Hawke sat in the driver's seat, working on getting the vehicle started but struggling with an engine that must have been flooded before the water subsided.

Arkady extended an arm, and a searing beam of light cut through the Humvee's front grill, bisecting the engine and popping the driver's side tire. The vehicle slumped at an angle and Hawke stared out the window, registering emotion for the first time since Shane had met him. He looked shocked.

Hawke raised a pistol and fired, barely missing Shane. Down the tunnel, the screams of the Waste echoed off the walls. It had heard the gunshot.

Arkady fired again, blasting the roof off the Humvee as Hawke ducked in the front seat, pushing the door open and scrambling away to avoid her attacks. The Burner was silent and efficient, if somewhat abrupt in her approach to combat. She needed better aim, unless she was toying with him on purpose.

The canyon floor lurched, and Shane lost his footing and stumbled against the wall. Rocks fell from above, and Hawke vanished in the fray for a moment before reappearing a few yards away from the Humvee, heading toward a narrow trail.

Shane ran through the shallow canyon river, making a beeline for the man. The rock face behind him collapsed a moment later, and Ventura cried out in surprise, dashing to the left to escape as a slab of stone the size of a bus crashed to the ground between the two men.

The ghosts and Ventura were on the far side, and more stones followed. Shane could do nothing but run after Hawke as the Waste burst from the canyon wall, destroying the old tunnel and burying everything in rubble.

Hawke looked back once, his eyes on the Waste and then on Shane. He turned and doubled his efforts, sprinting toward the path that led up the far wall and into the desert once more.

A blast of white fire cut through the Waste, severing arms that fell uselessly from the body, fading to nothing before they hit the ground.

The beast roared, turning toward what must have been Arkady. Its long, arm-like appendage wrapped around the bus-size boulder it had dislodged and lifted it like a great hammer. Shane briefly saw the ghost and the failures in the dust, glowing white, before the stone came down with earth-shattering force, launching debris like a bomb had gone off.

Shane followed Hawke up the path, gaining ground on the other man now that he was out of the water. The Waste bellowed and more lights flashed, but Shane did not look back. The ghosts were doing their job, taking on the monstrosity, and hopefully, Ventura was doing the same as he was, finding a route to escape.

A gunshot echoed through the canyon. Hawke had stopped, taking a shot at Shane, and narrowly missing. The sound drew the Waste's attention. The many faces turned and glared at Shane and Hawke, their mouths working to form gibberish words and screams.

The arm reached for Hawke and another blast of white fire cut a hole in the main body. The faces contorted in rage, and the monster returned its attention to the ghosts.

"I should have killed you when I had the chance," Hawke said. There was no malice in his voice. It was an observation.

"I've heard that before," Shane shouted back.

The Waste smashed the canyon walls, extending appendages to both sides and dragging rock onto the Humvees. Shane scrambled up the path toward Hawke as the many faces of the nightmare below shouted wild and hateful gibberish.

Hawke crested the ledge, hauling himself up as the rock shook beneath him and sheets of stone peeled away and fell into the canyon. He paused to steady himself for another shot at Shane but nearly lost his footing as more rock collapsed.

As Hawke rolled back to safety, Shane raced to the nearest ledge. He pulled himself up, hooking a leg over the edge of the rock even as he felt it loosening beneath him, and rolled quickly away as the ledge he had just been on slid into the canyon, dragging piles of rubble for a dozen yards in either direction with it.

"What did you do down there?" Hawke was not yelling but speaking loudly enough to be heard over the raging Waste as he approached Shane and kicked him in the gut.

Shane coughed, his body doubling over involuntarily after the powerful, surprising blow. Hawke kicked him in the shoulder as a follow-up and then stumbled back while the ground shook and cracked beneath him.

"I didn't do anything." Shane struggled to his feet and then resigned himself to racing on all fours away from the canyon's edge as more of the earth slipped away beneath them.

"The lead was never going to work," Shane shouted, avoiding the second landslide by mere feet. "It's not confined in the vault. It's not one thing anymore. You can never trap it."

"You have no idea what you're talking about." Hawke came at him again.

Shane caught the man's foot this time, cutting him off before he could land another blow. He rolled toward Hawke, using the shaking of the earth to force him to fall back.

"It's spreading. Like a goddamn cancer." Shane crawled up the other man's body. He punched Hawke in the face, breaking his nose. "It's all over the desert by now. If even one piece of it is free, it's all free."

"That's not how it works." Hawke growled and pushed the heel of his palm up under Shane's chin, thrusting his head back and forcing him off.

There was no sense in reasoning with the man. He was a person who thought he knew something, and no one was more obtuse than a man who thought he was right. Shane would have better luck getting through to the Waste.

Shane kept his left hand on Hawke's face, pushing down on his jaw and keeping his head plastered to the ground while he used his other to strike a series of blows against the other man's elbow until he could no longer keep his arm extended.

Hawke released Shane as his arm gave out. The soldier grunted and tried to twist free as Shane shifted his weight, forcing his elbow into the other man's throat and pushing down hard.

"What's in Lab Four?" Shane demanded.

Hawke struggled, flexing his jaw and blinking as he tried to draw in air. Shane put pressure on the man's carotid artery while he forced the same artery on the other side hard against the earth. The soldier was fighting to maintain consciousness.

"I don't... know..." He struggled to form the words. The Waste raged in the canyon just a stone's throw away, but Shane was not willing to let up on the man yet.

"They sealed it for a reason. Is it to keep ghosts out or in?"

"I don't know," Hawke choked out.

"Who does?"

Shane relented just barely, easing off the pressure on Hawke's throat enough to keep the man conscious and able to speak. Red-faced and sweaty, Hawke stared at Shane from the corner of his eye with half his face still buried in rock and wet sand.

"Nobody knows. There's not a goddamn person left alive who will ever talk to you or me. You think I'm here to take stock of these things? Protect them? I will destroy this entire goddamn desert if I have to. That's my job, Ryan. I'm here to make sure no one ever knows anything about what's out here. At any cost."

"Have you not figured this out yet, Hawke? You cannot destroy the Waste. Nothing you do will destroy it. We need something else."

"I've got something else," Hawke said and smiled for the first time, laughing into the dirt. "I've got something that will destroy everything."

CHAPTER 21
# LAB FOUR

Cold air swept across Shane in a wave, nearly freezing the water that saturated his clothing. Hawke's laughter stopped abruptly, and Shane turned in time to see the great, writhing tentacle made of arms and hands and other stray bits of flesh looming above them.

It crashed to the ground, each of the hands digging into the rock to take root, dozens of them grasping at anything they could hold on to. At the ruined canyon ledge, the throbbing trunk of the Waste's central body lurched up the wall. Gnashing teeth and wide eyes and screaming faces rose higher and higher, a wall of dead bodies weaved together in a bleeding, oozing tapestry.

Shane had no idea what had happened to Ventura or Arkady, but the Waste had given up on them to pursue him and Hawke. Its body oozed up the rock wall like a maggot, pulsing and squelching as it dragged itself after them.

Hawke must have had another bomb. It was the only thing that made sense, a final solution to clean up a mess that got out of control. Shane had seen something on the map, a Zero Point that corresponded to nothing else he had come across in the desert. It was centralized and had the potential to be the epicenter of a blast that would destroy every facility and wipe any trace of the experiments from the earth. Except the Waste, since it kept so much of itself hidden below ground. There was no guarantee a blast, even nuclear, would eliminate it. Not if it had hidden itself as far away as Benton.

Shane was up and running before the Waste's tower of screaming faces had pulled themselves fully over the canyon's ledge. He left Hawke to fend for himself and headed straight into the desert, leaving the canyon in his wake as fast as his feet would carry him.

The earth shook as the Waste raised its long, tentacle-like arm and swiped at Shane, missing him by just a few feet and slamming to the ground at his feet with force.

Shane looked back, taking a sharp left to avoid another strike, then zigzagging again. The Waste was big and powerful, but its movements were clumsy, and it didn't seem to track a moving target very well. Too many eyes in too many faces must have given it a poor perspective and made hunting difficult.

Hawke was fleeing as well, pacing Shane but heading at an angle that kept him parallel to the canyon. The Waste was torn between them and losing ground due to its indecisiveness.

The beast was fully out of the canyon as it lashed out at Hawke, leaving Shane. It lurched and moved like a broken thing struggling to maintain balance. It had lost pieces, maybe to Arkady or maybe to the thermite burning some of the skeletal remains that were parts of the multitude of haunted items that made up the whole. Whatever the case, it struggled more now than it had when Shane last saw it.

Underground, the Waste could tunnel at speed, but on the surface, it could only wriggle and lunge in fits and starts. It had formed an arm but not proper legs to carry its bulk. The result was an opportunity to outrun it. A chance for Shane to figure out what to do next.

The spirit wailed, and a light flashed in the dark. Shane saw Arkady above the canyon now with the failures and Ventura. They had found their way up, and the Burner was firing blasts of blinding white energy at the Waste.

The threat of damage was not enough to force the Waste back. Its many faces screamed, and the large appendage crashed to the ground but then whipped quickly right, sweeping the desert in an arc.

Sand and stone flew into the air, creating a blinding wall that concealed the Waste behind it like an impromptu smokescreen. The grasping hands found Hawke and took hold as they swept the desert floor.

Hawke made no noise. Shane saw the man go down and get dragged across the rocky desert floor. When the tentacle rose again, Hawke was suspended by his ankles, a half-dozen hands holding him aloft.

The ghost raised him like a child inspecting an insect, dangling the soldier in the air as the pulsing appendage retracted into the bulk of the main body, bringing him close to the multiple faces.

Hawke struggled to pull free, but more hands grabbed him and held him steady. He was restrained fully, arms and legs and more. The faces stared at him, screamed and shouted and growled. If he was replying, Shane was too far away to hear it.

The heads began to synchronize their wails, the muddy and irregular rhythm finding a cadence and a matched pitch until the Waste howled in tune, a single voice sounding like the mouth of hell had opened.

Shane gritted his teeth as the sound sent a shiver down his spine. It pierced his skull and made him want to run faster to escape from it.

The trunk of the Waste began to split. Faces tore apart from faces, flesh from flesh, with great ropes of melting fat, sinew, and organ tissue slopping from one side to the other as a chasm opened within it.

Bones protruded on each side of the hole, ribs and femurs and tibias and fibulas. They lined both edges as the flesh puckered and parted. Even at a distance, Shane understood right away what he saw. The Waste had made a mouth for itself, a massive, slavering, oozing maw with teeth made of bone and lips formed from swollen, raw flesh and organ meat.

Hawke's body was pushed into the mouth, and his scream was cut short as the mouth closed, slicing him in half. The tentacles dropped his legs and lower torso onto the ground while the mouth churned and chewed on the top portion.

The monster flesh repaired itself, making the Waste whole again, its mouth hidden within.

Ventura and Arkady ran toward Shane. The failures stumbled and swayed as they kept pace. They would reach Lab Four soon, maybe before the Waste caught up, but gaining access to it would take time.

Hawke's plan was not necessarily over. The man was dead, consumed by the Waste, but he must have had a contingency in place. Hawke would not have left things to chance. If he was willing to scorch the earth of everything including himself and his men, he would have made sure there was a way for it to still happen even if he was dead.

"There." Ventura pointed ahead and to the right as they caught up with one another.

Shane could not see what the other man was pointing to but followed. Coulson's ghost eyes were not hindered by the black, cloud-filled sky. He ran where directed, pacing his friend and pushing himself as hard as he could.

Ventura was drenched in sweat, and his face was red. Coulson was forcing his body as much as he dared and maybe more. Ventura was still alive and holding on, but he was being put through the wringer.

Arkady's white fire split the night, and Shane saw their destination in the flash, the shadow of something on the horizon, little more than a speck in the dark ahead of them. Lab Four awaited.

The Waste shrieked, and the ground thumped in a steady rhythm. It could not run above ground, but it lurched and pulled, reaching forward with its multiple arms again and again, slamming the ground with a great, thunderous boom each time it landed and pulled itself ahead.

"We need Arkady to get in there." Shane breathed heavily as his feet struggled through the wet sand.

He felt like he was running uphill with a pack on, his legs struggling for footing and gaining so little ground despite the effort. The wet desert was working against them, and they had such a small lead to begin with. They would need a distraction at the lab, something to keep the Waste busy for however long it took the Burner to melt the lead and find a way inside.

Ventura said nothing. Shane glanced at the other man and saw Coulson's eyes. The ghost nodded Ventura's head and fell back, taking the failures with him.

"Arkady, we need to get in there," Ventura yelled at the Burner.

He pointed into the darkness to where Lab Four waited and then stopped running, turning on his heels to face the Waste, flanked by the failures. Shane turned, watching the others fall back to block the path of the Waste as it lumbered after them.

White fire blazed through the night again, and the Waste bellowed in reply as Arkady burned another hole through its body. As Shane watched, the burned hole closed over like a healed wound, the ghostly flesh regrown as though nothing had happened.

He had thought the Burners were powerful enough to damage the Waste. But he was wrong.

Arkady's attacks were an inconvenience to the Waste, not a threat. It must have been like bug bites; something that gave it pause. The damage it had sustained earlier was probably from the thermite, and the loss of haunted items, but nothing happened to the ghost itself.

If the failures and Arkady were not strong enough to permanently harm the Waste, Shane and Coulson were the only options. Maybe Arkady could fight it hand to hand, and pull it apart in a way that any ghost could potentially harm another ghost. But how long would it stand still and allow such a thing from her or any of them? How could any of them even get close enough to cause serious damage?

The failures flickered to life next to Ventura, and Shane shielded his eyes. How would Coulson and Ventura survive?

Shane's instincts were to turn back, fight at their side, and do whatever they could for as long as they could. Even if they lost, they would go down fighting together. It was not in his nature to leave a man behind or let someone else fight in his place. But by the same token, he couldn't ignore their efforts to buy him time.

"Arkady!" he shouted, struggling toward Lab Four.

The ghost joined him, her face stern. She was not tired or slowed by the sinking sand. She raced ahead of him to the lead shell that covered their destination.

Shane raised his hand, covering his eyes as the ghost's fists burst to life. White-hot fire crashed against the lead shell of Lab Four. Behind them, the Waste howled, and a brighter flash of unfocused light lit the desert like the sun. One of the failures had fully ignited, and the Waste shrieked its discomfort at the attack. Shane tried to look back but could see only white. The failures and Ventura were lost in the blazing aura.

All that remained in the desert were the screams of a hundred faces, lost in the fury of nuclear fire from beyond the grave.

Shane covered his eyes and waited for it all to end.

CHAPTER 22
# THE UNSTOPPABLE FORCE

The Waste's many mouths screamed in unison, and Coulson felt Ventura's skin crawl. He wore the other man like a suit and controlled him like a puppet but left him in control of his mind to make sure the FBI agent didn't feel trapped and powerless. Coulson knew it was a horrible thing to be controlled. He was simply borrowing the living man's body and wanted to make sure he understood that.

Ventura, for his part, had given up autonomy with little resistance. Coulson had possessed people before, and it was not always a walk in the park. Ventura's exhaustion and abject fear made it easier. He didn't want to admit to that fear, to the panic he felt at the idea of dying, of being caught in the grasp of the monstrous Waste, but there were no secrets between ghost and man. Coulson would not judge him for the truths he found there.

Too many years inside other people's heads had put Thomas Coulson in a position to not judge others for even their darkest thoughts. Actions were what mattered. Ventura was doing what he could to save Shane Ryan and, in his mind, the world.

Shane continued running toward the lead-covered laboratory.

"Arkady, we need to get in there," Coulson shouted in Ventura's voice. He fell back, letting Shane continue to the destination, and signaled to the failures to hold back with him. He took a stand next to a stack of boulders nestled in gnarled weeds and trees.

His powers were slowly rebuilding. He was not his old self yet, still unable to maintain a fully convincing physical form, but he was getting better. While controlling Ventura allowed the living man to rest his mind and ignore the pain and damage to his body, it allowed Coulson a chance to build his reserves. It felt like a restful night's sleep, something the ghost had not enjoyed since his death.

The Burner went with Shane, and Coulson stopped, turning to face the Waste as it lurched after them.

"Light him up, guys." Coulson urged the failures forward. One of them sputtered, its lights flickering and then growing brighter like a light bulb with an inconsistent power supply. The other, the one Shane called Light Bulb, glowed softly and could grow no brighter.

*I think that one's tapped,* Ventura said inside his head. The other failure had done little since they'd acquired it. Light Bulb had lit the tunnels for them and maintained a bright glow when called upon. It might have simply been too far gone.

The Waste raged, and the glowing failure clicked, an audible pop that preceded a bright light bursting out in all directions. Coulson ducked behind the rocks, avoiding the scorching heat of the sudden explosive blast.

Light Bulb moaned, flickering softly but failing to achieve the results of its companion. It stumbled away, joining Coulson behind the rock as the other's light seared brighter and brighter, making the desert look like midday under a clear sky.

"You need to do something, buddy," Coulson said as Light Bulb collapsed next to him. He stared into the spirit's eyes, its empty sockets showing nothing but an empty skull with charred edges. Even so, there was still a sense of something there. Not much, not even thought, but feeling.

"I have an idea," Coulson said out loud.

*What?* Ventura thought.

"I need you to trust me and make some room," Coulson replied.

Ventura had no idea what that meant but sharing his head with Coulson was a two-way street of understanding. He could sense the ghost was withholding parts of himself, and did not invade too much, but when they worked together, it was like sharing thoughts in ways he had never imagined. He trusted Coulson as much as he had trusted anyone.

A short distance away, the Waste shrieked and shielded itself from the corona of the other failure's burst.

*Do it*, he thought without asking anything more.

Coulson controlled Ventura's hand and squeezed Light Bulb's arm. It sighed and was gone in an instant.

Ventura felt a rush and inhaled sharply. His muscles quivered across his body. He felt like he was going down rapidly on a rollercoaster, and cold, icy bursts of energy raked through his veins.

Coulson had pulled the failure and made it join them as a third party inside Ventura's body and mind. The new addition was nothing like Coulson. It did not think in sentences or even words. Ventura could barely even describe them as feelings so much as reactions. *Avoid this, do that, push the energy this way, focus thoughts that way.* It was like instinct, intuition clinging to the edges, just beyond full thought.

Even though the failure's mind was almost gone, the power it possessed was not. Ventura felt like he had been hit with a jolt of electricity. His body became alive with a buzzing acuity that made him feel like he could lift one of the boulders and hurl it across the desert or spring all the way to Las Vegas.

"Jesus," Coulson said softly.

*You feel that?* Ventura thought.

"That's the power of a spare soul added to the soup," Coulson explained.

He felt the energy in his veins, his muscles, the core of his being. It was pure adrenaline and set his mind racing.

They peered back toward Lab Four. Arkady had run ahead of Shane and was melting through the metal. It would take time to clear a path, enter the structure, and find a safe way in that wouldn't cook Shane. And then what? It could have been empty, or home to a worse monster. But no matter what awaited, waiting was the problem. It would take time.

"You ready?" Coulson asked.

*Ready as I'll ever be*, Ventura replied.

The Waste had stopped its progress. Hands and arms shielded the faces from the failure's light, but the ghost was flickering. It could not maintain the blinding, searing wall for any serious length of time.

Ventura was aware of the heat and the light the ghost produced but didn't feel it in any real way. It was as though a buffer had been placed between them, an invisible wall that absorbed the assault and protected his mortal frame from the ghost's energy. Coulson's doing, no doubt, fueled now by the energy of the failure that hung about silently in the back of his mind.

The failure's light continued to flicker as Ventura made his way around the rocks to face off against the Waste. He felt Coulson in his mind with him, working on something, needling at him like a memory he couldn't bring forth.

"Here goes nothing," Coulson said.

The failure sputtered and went dark. The ghost swayed, looking tired and sad, and then turned to face Ventura with its dead eyes. The Waste roared, lowering its many hands from the multiple faces.

Ventura reached out, and the failure took his hand. It was gone in a blink, pulled into the mix alongside its companion. Ventura gasped audibly, the rush of energy in his veins like pure lightning. He had never experienced anything like it, never imagined any experience could feel like it.

He screamed as the failure settled into the back of his mind, not in pain or fear or anger but just for release. Coulson and the two failures let loose within, four voices in one body, a more simple but organized version of everything the Waste had failed to become, howling into the desert over the exhilarating feeling rushing through them all.

The Waste replied, roaring in a hundred voices, and came at them in its single body. Ventura knew he should have felt fear. He should have willed his legs to move, but he did no such thing. He stood his ground instead. They had to buy Shane some time.

And that was what they would do.

When he had been alive, Coulson's greatest skill was his ability to know the unknowable. No one's mind was locked to him, and that afforded him great power. But it was not his only ability. More practical in the heat of the moment was his ability to move objects with his mind, to control them from across a room and not be bound by physical limitations.

As a ghost, it had never been entirely necessary to do such things. He could, if he wanted, walk through walls. Plus, he had little need for objects like keys or cups or shoes. He spent most of his telekinetic energy giving himself a body so that he appeared alive, and that was all that he needed to do. But that was before.

Fueled by the failures and his rising strength, Coulson reached into the recesses of his mind. The Waste's massive tentacle arm came crashing down on Ventura and hit the ground in front of the man with a deep, earth-shattering boom.

Ventura was forced to one knee, his hands extended above his head, and his fingers intertwined with two of the multitudes of hands that made up the nightmare arm. Other hands tried to claw at his flesh but could find no purchase. Coulson's mind pushed back on them.

The hands squeezed and tried to crush Ventura's, but the power running through his flesh and muscle swelled and resisted. Even as the great bulk of spiritual energy twisted and writhed to yank him aside, lift him, or force him down, he was an immovable object.

The Waste howled in frustration, and the many faces on the trunk of its incomprehensible body knotted their brows and scowled, puzzled and angry at their inability to wipe the man from the earth.

*How long can we hold this?* Ventura thought. It was impressive, but it was holding and nothing more. When he tried to move, stand, or force the Waste back, the tables turned, and he was rendered immobile. They were at a stalemate, each immobilized by the other.

"Surprised we lasted this long," Coulson whispered between clenched teeth.

Even at his full strength, back before everything that had happened, Coulson was not certain he had it within him to fight the Waste. He was channeling the power of two less powerful spirits, a living man, and himself. The Waste was more than a hundred souls. It was only by the grace of the mess that was its diffuse and incoherent mind that it had not crushed Ventura like a bug.

The real answer was that it didn't matter. They would hold it for as long as they could. He just hoped that Arkady was making some progress on the lead shell around the lab.

Because "as long as they could" would not be much longer.

# CHAPTER 23

# SECRETS HELD

Lead ran into the sand in white-hot rivers before it cooled to a scorching red, then orange, and finally black. Arkady's hands tore at it like she was peeling an orange, removing great handfuls of it and throwing it aside.

The Waste raged and fought with Coulson in the distance. The ghost, along with Ventura, had stopped it in its tracks. From the distance he was at, Shane had no idea how they had managed it, but they had exceeded any expectations he had. Now, he needed to hold up his end.

The Burner was tearing through another wall now, not just lead but steel and concrete. She had pierced through the shell and was breaking into the facility beyond. The hole she had created was not large, and melting metal kept falling into the way and needed to be cleared again.

"Freeze it and leave it; it's good," Shane said once he was confident the entrance was large enough.

Arkady peeled away a massive chunk of the wall as the edges melted and let her hands go dark. A cold air rose around them, and she concentrated, focusing on the skill all ghosts possessed, and sucked the heat from their surroundings.

The glowing metal dulled immediately, steaming and hissing into mist until at last, she nodded.

"I will help the others," she said. "I hope you succeed."

"Same." Shane ducked past her and hunched to fit into the narrow passage she had opened through the wall.

He was forced to pull out his lighter once inside. The interior of the lab was pitch-black and smelled old and stale. There was no char smell like the other labs, and nothing had been burned there save for the wall on his way in. The old smell was one he expected to find at a graveyard, earth and rot long since forgotten.

The light of the Zippo showed a single door, an elevator, with one silver button in a square panel. There were no stairs or options to go anywhere else. Shane pushed the button.

Old gears whirred to life. A tiny blue light appeared in the center of the button, and the elevator shaft hummed. Cables rattled, and the mechanism churned rhythmically as the elevator car rose to the top floor. It took only a few moments, and the door opened slowly.

Green-tinged fluorescent lights flickered and buzzed, struggling to turn on fully and not quite making it. The inside of the elevator was plain. A drab, gray tile floor was set below drab, gray wall panels. Shane stepped inside. Only one switch was set into the wall, a little silver button the same as outside. He pressed it, and the blue light came on. The doors closed, and the elevator rumbled as it descended back into the shaft.

The lights continued to flicker, and the ancient gears struggled and groaned as Shane was taken below. There were no other floors, or at least none that could be easily accessed through the elevator. There was only down to whatever secret the lab had held, hidden away for years.

The elevator stopped in a jerky shake. The car clunked into place, and the doors opened onto a hallway lit by the same flickering lights, half of which didn't work.

Ceiling panels made of cheap, acoustic tiles were either crooked or missing down the length of the hall, and someone had pulled wires loose, leaving bundles hanging from support beams.

There were marks on the walls, scratches from multiple hands. They were not deep, but they were clear and showed that someone had been either climbing the walls or struggling to break through them. Fingernails had scraped the paint loose in ragged, ugly streaks at random. It did not look like the work of ghosts.

Someone had been trapped down there once, long ago. A fine layer of dust covered everything, and the air was still. It felt almost invasive to Shane like he had stumbled on a place that no one was ever meant to discover. But he had no time to take in the details or wonder about its past. Ventura and Coulson were running out of time.

Shane crossed the hallway, avoiding the dangling wires and fallen roof tiles, and reached the only exit. The door was plain and old, a simple office door with a round, aluminum knob. He reached for it, his fingers touching the metal, and paused as a whirring sound above drew his attention.

Nestled in the corner where two walls and the ceiling came together, a nineties-era security camera extended its lens, focusing closely on Shane. He saw the aperture moving inside, zooming in to focus on his face.

The doorknob was cool under Shane's fingers. The camera lens whirred again, zooming out. There was nowhere else for him to go and no way to plan a different approach. He turned the knob, and the door fell open.

Shane expected a room like in the other labs, a small space with technical equipment, a computer terminal, or something of that nature. Instead, he was in a massive, industrial space full of metal catwalks and scaffolds around huge, metal turbines and humming engines that sprawled across a cavernous room.

Multiple machines painted red hummed and buzzed, emitting steam at irregular intervals along a network of thousands of pipes that led up and through the ceiling to parts unknown.

Water dripped freely from multiple places, and the room was a strange mix of hot and humid and freezing cold in bursts as a breeze from an unknown source cut through irregularly.

Though he had never seen any of the machines in the room, it reminded Shane of a power plant. He supposed it might have been a facility that powered the other labs. Maybe geothermal or some such, and it was still working after all this time. It didn't make sense in the location, so close to where so many nuclear tests had been conducted, but he was only guessing. Perhaps the tests had unearthed something they chose to exploit. But why seal it in lead while it was still running?

Banks and banks of control panels were lit with switches and dials. Catwalks laced the space, elevated above the numerous turbines and other machines set into the floor a half-level lower. Nowhere did anything move that Shane saw.

The room was empty of any signs of life, past or present. No spirits, and no bodies, either. No skeletal remains, scratches on the walls, or even handwritten notes or old coffee cups.

Shane stood upon a steel grate platform that extended the length of the wall in both directions away from the door, connecting to a half-dozen catwalks whichever way he looked. There had to be something more there. An office, at the very least.

He walked to the left, the metal ringing underfoot with each step. Ahead of him, he saw another knob extending from the wall. One single door led into a room opposite the entrance hallway.

The humming of the engines droned on. He was too deep in the earth to hear the Waste fighting with the others above. There was white noise from the machines around him and nothing more as he reached the unlabeled door.

The knob was colder than the first one, crisp like it had just come from the fridge. Shane lifted his head and looked around the room. There were a handful of scattered red lights along the walls, and security cameras monitoring the facility. Monitoring him.

He opened the door, and the cold air rushed out. Blessedly cold, given the smell that clung to the air. The lights buzzed and clicked, illuminating a new hallway that felt cramped and narrow.

Someone had pinned dead bodies to the walls the way an entomologist might pin up insects. Flayed, dissected, whole bodies and excised segments of others were held up by old wires torn from the front hallway ceiling.

Ribcages, split to show the heart and lungs inside, hung over skinned faces and severed hands. Across the hall was a full human skin from head to toe, cut away with careful precision so that almost none of it was torn beyond the neat, straight cuts.

Heads were mounted near the ceiling in rows like trophies for a hunter. Some had eyes, some did not. Some had flesh, others did not.

There were close to two dozen bodies. The floor was caked in blood, long since dried to a crusty, black film that must have been nearly two inches deep when it was new.

The bodies that still had flesh on them seemed partially mummified by the climate of the lab. They looked tough like jerky, and it was hard to discern if they had been shot, stabbed or beaten or anything of the sort.

Shane stared at the assorted corpses, the way they were displayed, and what was displayed. There were organs, whole limbs, and partial limbs, all placed with room to spare between them. They were organized and might have been considered neat if not for the bloody stains all around. Someone had taken time and thought to make the display. There was an example of nearly everything there, every individual part and organ. Everything that made a person, inside and out, was stuck to the walls of the hallway.

Shane's foot stepped on the old, dried blood. He tried to tread more carefully the second time, but it was no use.

*What difference does it make*, he thought. Someone was already watching him on camera.

As with the entrance, there was only one way out of the hallway. Not an elevator this time, just another forgettable office door, though this one was splattered with blood. The killing and dissecting had been done in the halls, and the bodies must have been hung where they fell. Though someone had cleared away the excess, the unwanted portions. Those were missing.

Shane proceeded to the bloody door. Inside were stairs, metal grates like the platform outside, that led down to the level where the machinery was located. Each step down created a noise, the metal ringing loudly under his weight until he reached the bottom. The floor there was concrete, and the space was like a storage area, with pipes running across the ceiling and shelves of light bulbs, gaskets, tubing, and other supplies on the far wall.

The air grew warmer as he proceeded down the narrow cement passageway at the bottom of the stairs. At the end of it was another door, this one labeled "security".

Shane pulled the door open, and a smell like sweat and meat rolled out. The room was warm and illuminated only by the monitors that covered the left wall. Security camera footage of the facility was being fed in, but some monitors also showed the desert. Most showed nothing but static, but Shane saw Doomtown, a guard post, and even Hawke's base.

In the corner of the room, a sickly, yellow-brown light flickered. Flames danced over a pile of twisted body parts, and for a moment, Shane thought he was looking at the Waste until it became clear that it was only a small portion, a segment like the one he had discovered in a tunnel before.

The parts moved, shifting like a coiled snake unfurling itself. The fire continued its slow, dull burn, the color of old pus and bile. A head lifted to face Shane, and then a second and a third. They hung limply, stared dully, and made no sound as arms braced themselves against the walls to rise higher, climbing like a centipede until one central face, protruding away from the others, smiled gleefully as hands sneaked in from behind it to cover its mouth.

"You're here!" it said in a hushed and joyful whisper.

"He's here!"

"Here!"

"He's here!"

The other heads echoed the first, each one sounding relieved or ecstatic. There was perhaps a dozen, and many more arms, but little else to the spirit's body. It was like the Waste, but in fuller possession of its faculties.

"Welcome!" the central head said, the hands spreading to either side of the face as it approached Shane, beaming as tears filled its eyes.

# CHAPTER 24
# THE JOYFUL THING MADE OF HATE

The centipede-ghost scurried toward Shane, and he took a step back. His reaction caused it to pause, and the smiling face was briefly confused. Fleshless skulls wreathed the smiling face like a necklace, and its eyes were rimmed by bulging blisters. The other heads only focused on Shane sometimes, averting their eyes when he looked back, and whispering softly to one another.

There was part of a torso still attached to the central head, but it was fused into a mishmash of other shoulders and arms below.

Shane counted eleven heads, not including the skulls, and arms from fifteen bodies. Relatively speaking, it was a small thing compared to the Waste, but the parts together made it the size of a large man.

The faces were of men, women, and a handful beyond recognition. Most had been burned, but not directly. They bore the wounds of steam burns or some indirect heat that caused severe blistering, swelling, and weeping redness. There was no char on the edges, but on a few, the flesh looked as though it had been boiled so long that the bone was exposed.

Most astonishing was it could focus on Shane and speak coherently, something the Waste hadn't come close to doing. Despite the happiness and the excitement it displayed at seeing Shane, he was still very much aware of the bloody hallway he'd passed through.

"Who are you?" he asked.

"A friend," the ghost replied, its tone gushing and dramatic. "Oh, what a friend I could be to you."

The spirit's mouth smiled too wide, and it took Shane a moment to realize the problem was that its lower jaw did not belong to the upper jaw. A second head had been fused to the top part, giving the spirit a much larger mouth than it should have had.

"My name is Dr. Shaw," the ghost said. "Your good friend, Dr. Shaw."

The central head nodded encouragingly, and it reminded Shane of the way people spoke to babies or pets.

"Shaw!"

"The good doctor."

"Friend!"

The other heads added their two cents, always more softly than the head that belonged to Shaw. Shane recognized the name: He had heard it from Arkady. She said he had run the project. He had made the Burners and the Waste. She wanted to kill him, but it seemed she was too late.

"What is your name, friend?" Shaw asked.

The hands that came from behind his head reached out again, and more of those that supported the bulk of the spirit did the same. It reminded Shane of images he'd seen of people in crowds, reaching up to celebrities, desperate to touch them or even just be acknowledged.

"Shane." He kept his distance. "Have you been watching everything?"

He nodded to the monitors, and Shaw's face smiled its too-big smile and the head nodded. Other heads nodded and spoke their approval.

"We watch," one said.

"We see."

"Then you know what's up there right now," Shane said.

Shaw nodded, and other heads, those with the range of motion, nodded as well.

"We see it, yes." Shaw gestured to the monitors and drifted toward them. "We see the world from down here. It comes to us through wires and machines."

"Wires and machines!"

"The computer shows us the world."

"The world we lost."

Shane looked below the security monitors at the old IBM desktop computer sitting there, an Internet Explorer window opened to a page about military facilities in America.

"The internet. You have the internet?" Shane said, almost laughing.

"Yes. Yes!" Dr. Shaw replied. "We have watched the world and learned for years."

"Years," several other voices repeated.

"So much to see."

The ghost seemed so genuinely excited by the prospect of talking to Shane. It could be easy to forget what he had seen upstairs, what Shaw had done, and what he might be capable of doing. Someone had sealed him into the lab for a reason.

He wondered what a ghost, trapped with a computer for decades, could have learned about the world. It must have been late-nineties internet, a slow dialup connection, giving the spirit news and images at a snail's pace.

The ground shook, a distant rumble and a reminder of what waited outside.

"Were you made like the Waste?" Shane asked.

"Waste…?" A dreamy confusion appeared on Shaw's face.

"Waste!"

"What waste?"

"The ghost outside. The one made of many," Shane explained.

"Marlowe." Shaw nodded, and the other heads nodded and agreed with enthusiasm.

"It's Dr. Marlowe."

"He means Marlowe," they said.

"Who is Dr. Marlowe?" Shane asked.

The hands reached around Shaw's face and covered his mouth. His eyes were wide, and the effort strained the blistered flesh until it looked like they might pop.

"Oh, he's a very bad man," Shaw said. He shook his head and looked scared. His tone, his expression, all of it was theatrical.

"Villain!" one of the others added.

"He's dangerous. You should stay away from him."

The heads all agreed that Marlowe was terrible without specifying why or who he was.

"He's part of the Waste?" Shane asked.

"He made it. He's responsible," Shaw said.

"Yes, he caused it."

"He's a murderer."

"He was the one behind the experiment?" Shane asked.

"Oh yes," Shaw replied. "I was his assistant. You see what he did to me. How he burned me and ruined me and made me into a monster."

"Monster," the others agreed.

"We are a monster."

Shaw nodded, the other heads nodded, and there was a pleading quality to all their voices. They wanted Shane to agree with them. They wanted him to feel sympathy for them. Something about the ghost's demeanor made Shane doubt the story.

"How did Marlowe end up like he is?" Shane asked.

"It was me," Shaw said proudly. "I did it to him. I had to hide him away. Hide us away!"

"We had to hide."

"To be safe!"

"Marlowe was the real monster, Shane. Marlowe is evil, and I was controlling him. I was going to destroy him. We were one."

"We were one!"

"We were free once."

"I don't understand what you're saying," Shane said.

"We were made to be one. To fix the whole. And we used to be one, but we were broken. Marlowe tore us away and became uncontrollable."

"A monster," the others said.

"And we wanted to stop him, but you see him. He is so strong. Stronger now. Bigger than before. He was too strong for us. He was body. We were mind. And so, we imprisoned him. It was our idea. To keep the world safe, you see. Hidden away in a vault of lead. So safe."

"We saved the people," a voice said.

"We saved souls."

"So you did this to yourself? To join the Waste and control it? Or did Marlowe accidentally create you?"

"No!" Shaw shook his head. The others vigorously rejected the notion as well. "On purpose. He made us on purpose to be powerful. To be so powerful."

"So much power," another voice added.

"We were so strong."

"So we sacrificed ourselves to be here and trap him there," Shaw explained.

"A sacrifice," the heads said.

Shaw looked disheartened, and his head drooped. The hands kept reaching for him, and those around his face hung limp.

"You freed yourself from the Waste, took the brains, and left the brawn," Shane said. Shaw nodded, agreeing that this was indeed what happened. "But who imprisoned you?"

"The others!" Shaw said. "They misunderstood. They thought we were evil like Marlowe. They trapped us here and sealed us away by mistake."

"Mistake," a voice whispered.

"It needs to be destroyed, not imprisoned," Shane said. "It's grown too powerful."

"Yes!" Shaw agreed. The vigorous nodding from every head

confirmed they were all on board with Shane's assessment. "Marlowe should be destroyed. He's a danger to everyone. We can help."

"Let us help."

"Let us out," the heads urged.

"We tried, you see. The computer!" Shaw's eyes were wide, and he gestured at the machine.

"The computer!"

"We found friends there!"

"We used it," Shaw continued. "To find Bennet Ross. To open the vaults. To send them to Project Five. To set everything in motion. And now, you are the final piece."

"The last piece!"

The hands reached for him, and the faces pleaded with urgency. He needed a weapon to fight the Waste. He had gone into the lab to find it, but Shaw was not his weapon. He needed to get back up before it was too late for Ventura and Coulson.

Shane took a step back, and the heads around Shaw let their eyes drift to the door. The sickly yellow fire that seemed to ooze from the ghost grew brighter and stronger, and the hands began to slowly turn. They switched to positions better suited for grasping.

"We can help you," Shaw said quietly. None of the other heads spoke. The eyes were either fixed on Shane or on the door.

"Why did they seal you in here if you had the ability to explain yourself? Why wouldn't they want you to help?" Shane asked, his suspicion growing.

He took another step back and was in the hallway now.

"They were confused. Because of how we look," Shaw said. "They treated us like a monster."

"Monster," another one whispered.

Shane took another step and then Shaw took a step as well, using several hands and arms to close the gap between them as the twisted body approached the door. Shaw craned his neck, looking over Shane's shoulder to the hallway and the stairs behind him.

"Tell us, Shane… how did you get in here?"

"How?"

"How do we get out?"

Most of the security monitors were dead. Any cameras outside of the lab would have been destroyed by the lead. Shaw could not see what happened up top, and he would have no idea how Arkady got Shane inside.

"I came in from the surface. Took the elevator." Shane backed away another step.

Once again, Shaw mirrored his movements. The ghost filled the doorway now, some of the hands clutching it for stability. The other heads looked up and around the hallway, past Shane, toward the stairs. Their eyes lit up.

"But there's lead, Shane," Shaw said, so softly now that he could barely be heard. "Lead is repellant to us. Anathema. It cannot be crossed."

"Cannot be crossed," the others whispered.

Shane stepped back again, and Shaw braced himself in the doorway, hands extending all around, clutching at the wood and concrete. Only Shaw's eyes remained on Shane. The other heads were all staring up.

"How did you get inside our nest?"

Shane turned on his heels and ran. Shaw clambered up the wall like a spider, his many hands gripping and clutching until he reached the ceiling and the multiple pipes there. The spirit moved hand over hand, suspended upside-down above Shane as it raced him to the end of the hall and the waiting staircase, then scaled the wall.

Shaw reached the door at the top of the stairs while Shane was only halfway there, dropping to the steel grate platform and barring the way.

"You've done so much for us," the ghost said.

"Freedom," the others sang out.

"When you die down here, I want you to know how grateful we are.

How joyful you have made us!"

"Thank you!"

"Thank you, Shane!"

There were tears in Shaw's eyes as he smiled a wide and crooked smile, and then he turned and raced down his hall of corpses.

# CHAPTER 25
# THE HORRIBLE DEAD

Shaw moved impossibly fast on his many arms. Shane ran after him, out onto the platform and toward the hallway that led to the elevator. Something above boomed, and the faint hint of a vibration echoed in the chamber full of machines, but Shane ignored it.

He raced after the ghost, heading down the hall toward the elevator. Shaw was there, the door opening for him. The many faces moaned, crying out in elation, and their hands clasped together in praise.

Shane said nothing as he closed the gap. One of the heads mounted crooked behind Shaw's saw him in its peripheral vision and turned awkwardly to look at him, alerting the ghost to his presence.

Shaw braced himself in the elevator doorway and rotated backward and upside-down to position the numerous arms closer to Shane as he approached. Shane got one swing in, one blow to the crooked head that spotted him, with enough force to dislodge a tooth before a dozen hands grabbed him.

The ghostly faces wailed in pain and anger at Shane's assault. Hands lifted him from the ground by his wrists; others wrapped around his throat and clawed at his face. They pushed his mouth open and probed inside while others clawed at his eyes, nose, and ears.

"You need to rest, Shane," Shaw told him.

"Sleep."

"Leave!" the others said.

"You have helped us so much. Stay here now. Use the computer; it will show you the world. It will show you our triumphs in the days to come.

You are our savior, so that is your gift. Witness our rise, Shane! Know that it is all because of you!"

The arms hurled Shane backward, throwing him halfway down the hall before propelling Shaw and the rest of his mangled, fused pieces into the elevator. Shane was on his knees, preparing to stand and come after the ghost as the elevator door closed. Shaw's grinning face was the last thing Shane saw.

The gears and motors within the elevator shaft began to work and buzz the way they had when Shane arrived. Cursing, he grasped the edge of the elevator door and pulled. He needed to work on it, creating some tension and getting a grip just with his fingertips before he opened the gap big enough to fit a hand inside and pry the door open. The shaft was empty save for some cables. Above him, the elevator car rattled to the surface.

There was no ladder or access shaft alongside the elevator. If he was to leave again, he'd be taking the same route as Shaw. He had to wait.

Ventura felt the air on his face, the rush of a swift, cool breeze, and it made him squint. A brief sensation of freedom overwhelmed the panic. He was in the air, arms wide, stone and sand vanishing beneath him as he sailed away from his place in front of Lab Four into the distance.

The Waste had swung its massive tentacle arm and clipped him from behind. Coulson's power had absorbed the shock of the blow, which might have otherwise broken his spine, but the ghost could only alter the physics of a living human body so much. The force of the blow had to go somewhere, and it sent them flying.

"Brace yourself," Coulson said, using Ventura's voice.

They hit the ground and rolled across the damp sand and stone. The ghost buffered Ventura from the blow again, taking as much damage as he could, but it still hurt. The burn on his back was becoming harder to ignore. Ventura didn't know if that was because Coulson was losing his ability to conceal it or if the pain was just becoming too much for him to handle. He didn't want to ask.

Arkady blasted the Waste with more fire as she ran across the desert. She had to keep on her toes to avoid the counters from the monstrous spirit. If it caught her, it would consume her, so standing still was not an option. It limited her ability to assist, but at least she was still with them.

Shane had vanished. He'd been inside the lab for what seemed like forever. Ventura knew it was minutes, probably no more than twenty at this point, but those were twenty long minutes they'd dealt with the Waste.

Coulson had held it at bay for more than half that time, keeping it at a stalemate, but its relentless assaults broke through his barriers, and he was forced to scale back his defenses to protect Ventura's body. They could not fight much longer.

The Waste had become distracted by its inability to kill Ventura. Though there was no way to communicate with it or even understand what it might be thinking or feeling, he was certain it was frustrated. Every failed attack made it rage, and sometimes, it would not simply attack Ventura again, instead slamming its massive tentacle appendage into the earth, breaking the ground, and hurling rocks before returning to its target.

Arkady was a constant nuisance like a bee buzzing around the Waste, stinging and fleeing again and again to keep it from focusing on Ventura and Coulson. They had fallen into a rhythm of distraction that bought Shane time until an unexpected swipe of the arm sent Ventura flying.

The Waste bellowed and thundered toward where he had landed, legs and arms and torsos crunching the earth like the treads of a beastly flesh tank. Ventura scrambled to his feet, the energy of Coulson and the two failures surging through his flesh, and ran to avoid another strike.

Ventura headed toward the lab and the entryway that Arkady had made for Shane. The Burner was already there, firing off another stream of white light from her hands to force the Waste back and give Ventura some room.

"He's coming back." Arkady stole a peek behind her to the lab. "The elevator is coming back up."

Ventura felt a palpable relief, not just his but Coulson's as well. If they were going to defeat the Waste, they needed Shane's help. Whether or not he found something in the lab to help didn't matter anymore. They couldn't handle it on their own.

Ventura knew he should have been exhausted and sore. As he ran, feeling his legs pumping and the adrenaline going through his veins as the Waste raged and gave chase, he knew nothing he did should have been possible. Everything he had accomplished was because of Coulson. If Ventura survived, he would owe the ghost his life.

"Ryan!" Coulson yelled using Ventura's voice as they approached the lab. "Hope you dragged a miracle out from down there."

He saw Arkady staring into the hole she had melted through the lead shell. The ghost's expression dropped, and she stumbled backward, wide-eyed fear on her face. Ventura had rarely seen such a reaction from the dead. It was the kind of fear the living expressed when they saw a ghost for the first time. Seeing it on the Burner's face was shocking enough to stop him in his tracks.

An arm reached out from the darkness within the previously sealed laboratory. A pale, white hand covered in ugly, amber blisters gripped the edge of the metal. A second hand joined it, this one with a darker complexion and a missing thumb. Then a third hand, a fourth hand, more and more until the entrance was circled in hands like a dozen people were reaching through at the same time.

A face emerged from the center of the hands. It was a man's face, grinning from ear to ear with an uneven and strangely wide jaw. Blisters covered the spirit's flesh, and his eyes gazed out at the world, the sky, the horizon, Ventura, and the Waste behind him with a look of joy.

"We are free!" the ghost shouted.

"Free!"

"Freedom!" multiple voices chimed in simultaneously.

The many faces of the Waste wailed a sound unlike any Ventura had heard. The pulsating, writhing trunk rose like a serpent as the many-armed ghost pulled itself free from Lab Four.

More heads appeared, and the ghost shifted its position, so the arms hung below it like the tentacles of a squid. The central head sat atop pale shoulders, and more heads ringed it around the rear of the body. It looked as though the main head was wearing a ceremonial crown made of other faces.

"Oh, Marlowe!" The ghost ignored Ventura and stared up at the Waste. His many arms reached up, palms spread as though welcoming the Waste in for a hug. "I've come back for you."

*What the hell is this?* Ventura thought.

"Not a clue," Coulson said. "Where's Shane?"

The many-faced ghost headed toward the Waste, but the larger spirit became uneasy. For the first time, Ventura watched as it pulled back, its huge body roiling and lurching to one side to keep a distance between itself and the spirit that spoke to it.

"Did you forget me, old friend?" the smaller ghost asked.

"Remember us!"

"Join us!"

The heads all spoke, some softly, some shouting, but all deferred to the main head. The Waste's faces bellowed and cried out. It looked confused, frightened, or angry. The tendril of arms rose, and Ventura thought it might attack the newcomer, but it held off.

Ventura moved around the smaller spirit, ignored now by both it and the Waste, and joined Arkady outside of the lab.

"What is that thing?" Coulson asked her when they were at her side.

"It's Shaw," the Burner said softly. "It's Dr. Shaw."

Ventura remembered the name and remembered what she said he had done. But he was something different now. He had done to himself what he had done to the Waste, or something close to it. His ability to speak made him unique, but he surely could not have wanted whatever had happened to him.

*Is this Shane's weapon?* Ventura asked.

"No," Coulson said softly. Shane was not in the elevator. Only Shaw had emerged.

"Come back to me, Marlowe! Let me take control again!" Shaw yelled up at the beast.

The Waste howled, and the faces tried to form words but nothing intelligent came out. Shaw moved toward it again, and that was when the Waste's patience suddenly ended.

With a deep, angry groan, the tentacle of arms came crashing down on Shaw. The ghost and its many heads cried out in protest, but the appendage slammed them to the earth.

The Waste moved in a fury, coiling around on itself and dragging Shaw closer. It was too hard to see what was happening, but the spirit was too close. Ventura backed into the opening of the lab, watching from the melted access hole.

A shriek arose from the Waste, and it unfurled. Shaw had attached himself to its trunk, to the many faces, using his multiple hands to dig into the Waste's body. They ripped and tore the flesh apart like they were tunneling, and the multiple heads pushed into the flesh chasm they had made.

The Waste tried to pry Shaw free, but its appendage was too slow and clumsy compared to the smaller spirit. Soon, the heads and arms were gone from sight, and the Waste shuddered, rising to its full length like a charmed snake going higher and higher.

The heads screamed, and the appendage wrapped around itself, coiling about the main body. The screaming stopped abruptly, every mouth silenced as one, and then, as though in slow motion, the Waste collapsed.

Arkady ducked into the lab alongside Ventura. The impossibly large mass of congealed spirit parts fell to the ground like a tree cut off at the base. It landed with a powerful thud and then… nothing.

The sound of Ventura's breathing filled his ears. Arkady at his side made no sound, nor did Coulson or the failures in his head. The sudden silence of the Waste was off-putting. It was as though the entire desert had died. There was nothing to hear.

The ghost appeared to have died, but of course, that was not possible. If it had been destroyed, it would have vanished. Instead, it was incapacitated. It didn't make sense.

*We should do something*, Ventura thought. They would never get a better time to act.

"I don't think we want to go out there," Coulson whispered.

Arkady looked at him but then refocused her attention on the Waste as the spirit released a long, deep exhale from all its mouths at once. The tentacle appendage twisted and rolled then pushed down on the ground, lending stability to the whole as it forced itself up again.

The trunk of the ghost had changed. The torsos, heads, and random mishmash of body parts were moving. Even the tentacle appendage was pulling back into the main body. Flesh squelched and tore as the Waste rearranged itself.

Hands pushed Shaw's face out of a churning, throbbing mass of unidentifiable flesh. More hands pushed those hands, and it was as though his head was rising upon a stem of arms.

Other heads formed joints like knees or shoulders, clusters of them that capped off new appendages formed first of the torsos, abdomens, and chests, then legs and arms.

Multiple support appendages, burst through the sloppy, festering flesh down the length of the enormous thorax of the Waste. Six legs, eight, then a dozen, while more thick and pulsing tissue rose around Shaw's face. He was the center now, his crooked, smiling face unsettlingly small against the bulky backdrop of the rest of the ghost.

"Come to me, friends!" Shaw yelled, staring at the entrance to the lab. "Come and join me!"

"Join us!"

"Be with us!"

A hundred voices screamed their encouragement and desire to make Ventura and Arkady a part of the Waste.

"Jesus, where the hell is Ryan?" Coulson said.

Then, the monster began to move.

# CHAPTER 26

# THE MONSTER

Arms twisted about each other like vines and reached out toward the lab. Ventura backed up as the writhing and ever-growing limb reached through the hole in the wall, four hands at the end grasping at him.

He backed away quickly, making for the elevator, and mashed the button on the wall. Gears hummed and churned inside, but the door did not open. There was no other way to escape.

"Shield your eyes," Arkady said.

Ventura covered his face with his arm, and he felt a blast of heat fill the enclosed space. Even with his face covered, the red glow penetrated enough to see that she had flared her power toward the entrance.

The Waste screamed in a hundred voices, but they were organized now. They screamed as one, and the ground outside shook.

"Why would you fight me?" Shaw shouted. He sounded genuinely shocked, concerned even, and the other voices joined him a moment later, questioning the actions of those in the lab.

The arm was gone, destroyed by Arkady's attack. The temperature in the cramped space had risen significantly with just one use of her power. She could not hope to fight the Waste, or whatever it was now, from inside.

"When you join us, you will understand." Shaw's voice boomed like thunder. "Once you're a part of us, you will see everything."

"Be with us!"

"Join us!"

Then the lab shook, a fearsome vibration that threatened to knock Ventura over. The Waste was up against the outer wall now, one of the arm-like appendages looped into the opening once more but this time not searching and grasping. Instead, it clutched lead and steel and concrete, tearing the wall off.

Metal groaned, and concrete shattered. What had been a small hole, just big enough for a human to enter, broke apart, leaving a space twice as big. Shaw's face appeared, thrust into the entrance.

"Join us, dear friends. You have no idea how fun it is! The togetherness, the joyful oneness."

He tore away more of the lead to get deeper into the lab. Ventura held his breath. He felt Coulson and the others in his mind and knew no one had any idea of how to proceed. Arkady could continue blasting her fire, but it had proven no good at destroying the Waste, only slowing it down. Now that it had merged with whatever Shaw was, there was no guarantee it would even do that.

Xander Ventura was going to die. He was as sure of that fact as he had been of anything in his life. He had been backed into corners before, and he'd risked his life in the line of duty, but he'd always felt that there was always a chance of coming out on top, no matter how slim. That feeling was gone now. That hope was gone. The Waste was beyond such things.

Behind them, the elevator rattled to a stop. Ventura gasped audibly, turning his head to face the doors. There was still a chance to get out.

The doors opened, and flickering green light filled the space. Shane Ryan stood in the center of the elevator car and scowled as he watched the many hands of the Waste yank another segment of the lead shell off the building's exterior.

"You are supposed to watch, friend!" Shaw sounded confused as he loomed over the hole he had created.

Shane looked at Arkady.

"Can you get rid of him?"

"I can try," the ghost said. "Close your eyes."

Shane looked at Ventura and nodded, covering his eyes as the Burner ignited, firing a blast so bright Shane thought it would sear his retinas even with his eyes closed.

Shaw screamed, and the many heads screamed with him. Not just his, but those of the Waste, joined in sharing their pain and displeasure.

"Jesus, he took control of the Waste?" Shane said as the light flared out.

"He seems to be the brains," Ventura confirmed.

"He dissected everyone that was left down there with him. Plastered their parts on the wall like art. Tried to sell it to me like he was another victim. But his story didn't add up. He's as crazy as the Waste was, just smarter."

"Do you know how to fight it?" Ventura asked.

Coulson was letting him speak, either because he wanted to ask the same question, or because he already knew Shane's answer.

"No," Shane answered. "I have no idea."

Ventura's disappointment showed on his face, but Shane had no time to worry about the man's feelings. If they got into the elevator, they could force the Waste to follow, and maybe something below could help contain it. There had to be something.

"Shane." It was Coulson speaking.

"We should get Ventura down—"

"No." Coulson turned to look back at the monster. "I have an idea, but you're not going to like it."

Two arms came down, groups of hands grasping the edges of the hole. Arkady fired upon them, but more arms took their place. Her fire scorched the already burned flesh, and cut through it slowly, but extra arms and hands took over the moment one was crippled. The lead shell cracked more, and the roof of the lab peeled off to reveal the black, cloud-filled sky.

"We don't have time," Shane said.

"Let me in."

They stared at each other for a beat as the screaming of the Waste filled the night around them.

"What?" Shane asked.

"Let me take control. Just this once. Ventura is exhausted. Forcing him to go on…" Coulson finished his sentence with a shake of Ventura's head.

Shane gritted his teeth. He did not want Coulson to possess him. But he also did not want to risk Ventura's life further. Neither did he want to be consumed by Shaw and the Waste. He would not become a part of that monster if there was any way he could prevent it.

"Do it. But this better work."

"I need you to brace yourself. It's going to get crowded."

Shane exhaled loudly. The Waste howled as Arkady blasted it again.

Ventura slumped against the wall next to the elevator, and Coulson rose from him like he was creeping out of the shadows. The two failures came with him, and Ventura coughed loudly. He offered Shane a weak smile and then closed his eyes, falling unconscious.

The walls ripped off the lab. The Waste had encircled the building with its serpentine body, and no matter where Arkady fired, other portions were free to tear down the walls and expose those inside.

"Go!" Shane shouted.

Coulson reached for him, but there was resistance.

"You gotta relax," Coulson urged.

"This entire situation is not relaxing," Shane growled.

He tried to clear his mind, tried to ignore the cold desert wind, the howls of the Waste, and the blinding, burning flashes of light. And he tried to let the ghost of Thomas Coulson merge with him.

He felt cold. The cold spread up his arm like ice water being injected into his veins. Then the cold moved in a rush. Shane felt it pulling into the core of his being like water down a drain. It filled him, seeping into his core and clinging to an unseen part of him.

"Yes." Coulson sounded relieved. The voice was not outside but inside. He was in his mind, fully a part of Shane. It was unpleasant and uncomfortable in every way, but Shane ignored it.

"You two, come." Coulson spoke in Shane's voice.

The failures responded without question, each of them drifting into Shane. With Coulson's aide, there was no resistance. The spirits piled in, occupying a spot in the back of Shane's mind. They felt like strangers in the back of a room looking at him, giving him the feeling of being watched even though they were doing nothing.

"Arkady, we need you here," Coulson yelled in Shane's voice.

The Burner's fists were still blazing, and she turned, looking back at him.

"Shaw will kill you!" she replied.

"He'll try." Coulson took Shane's body to her side. "You ready to kick it up a notch?"

Arkady stared into Shane's eyes, seeing something there. She nodded and reached for him. Shane took her hand, and she was gone.

Ventura was passed out, his breathing shallow, and his body well beyond its limits. Only Shane remained. But he was more than he had been.

Four spirits filled Shane's mind and body. He felt each distinct presence like a cold hand on his shoulder. It was unlike anything he had ever endured.

"One last thing," Coulson said.

*What?* Shane replied.

"I need everything I've got to hold this together. You're in the driver's seat."

Shane felt Coulson relinquish control of his body. His arms and legs were his again, and his voice could speak his words. The ghosts were a part of him like a feeling in his bones that set his teeth on edge and made his muscles twitch.

"Your friends are a disappointment to me, Shane. But they will still join us. Everyone will join us," Shaw said.

Without Arkady's attacks, there was no longer anything to hold him back. The ghost loomed over Shane and then dropped, the many arms spreading wide and welcoming as they reached out to pick him up.

"Join us!"

"Join the one!"

Shaw's crooked mouth fell open, his smile sagging into a slack-jawed, dumbfounded stare, and then it opened wider and wider. The flesh at the sides of his jaws stretched, and his broken mouth gaped wider and wider.

The ghost's throat smelled like rotten meat, and was lined with tears and sores. It looked to have been stitched together with whatever ragged bits of flesh didn't fit the exterior it had crafted, and in the middle of it was a pulsing gullet lined with teeth and lips and bony protrusions. It was wide enough to swallow a man whole.

Shane stood still and waited. Shaw drew close, mouth agape, intent on devouring him.

Without a word, Shane swung. His fist smashed into the side of Shaw's face with a force that shocked even him. Ghostly flesh tore as bones shattered like glass inside the spirit's face. There was not enough strength to offer any resistance. Shane's fist pierced Shaw's jaw and tore it loose from his skull, shredding his neck down to his chest and the ring of skulls he wore like a necklace.

The oversized jaw crumpled and tore away from the ghost. Shaw screamed but could no longer make words,

"What have you done?" the other heads demanded.

"What did you do?"

"Why?"

Strength flowed through Shane like he had been charged, wound tightly with a key, and finally sprung loose.

He rushed from the lab and at the Waste as it reeled in surprise and uncertainty. Shane's hands grasped wrists and elbows and fingers and more. He pulled the ghost apart, tearing flesh and throwing anything and everything aside. The pieces shuddered and fell apart, none of them making it to the ground.

"No!" the many voices of the Waste screamed at once.

The appendages came down on him, the insectoid legs made of hands and feet and more. They stabbed at him and tried to crush him, but he caught them, pulled them asunder, and sent the pieces flying into the night to be forgotten.

He reached one of the other heads, a pasty face with half of the flesh missing, threatening him with pain untold. He punched a hole through it, and it exploded, creating a larger hole in the Waste's body. The blowback washed over Shane like it was nothing.

As more heads exploded and more pieces of the Waste fell away, unhealed and unreplaced, the beast began to understand. Soon, it was not attacking but defending. It tried to force Shane away, to block his attacks, but anything it put in his way was ripped to pieces.

Too many legs fell away from the central trunk, and soon enough, the Waste could no longer hold itself up. It collapsed, writhing, and struggling on a trunk made of torsos, errant spines, partial thighs, and too many heads to count. Shane broke them all.

The great monstrosity was reduced to a wriggling, crippled, aimless thing. Shane destroyed every piece he found until at last, he came across what remained of Shaw's head, the still hands covering it. With the lower jaw gone, he just stared into Shane's eyes.

He saw fear in the ghost's pleading and desperate eyes. Shaw was scared of being destroyed. Even after everything he had done, from years past to right then, he didn't understand. He couldn't understand.

Shane crushed Shaw's skull. It popped in his hand like a water balloon, and the energy it released tore a hole through the back of the remaining body that quickly shredded every fiber of ghostly flesh. Nothing remained. The Waste was gone.

The energy in Shane's body had not dissipated. He felt like he could have taken on five more Wastes or sprinted all the way to Vegas. He could have punched a hole in a mountain.

"Get out," he said sharply. "Now."

The power was not something he wanted. It was not something anyone should have had, and he didn't like what he had to trade to get it. Four ghosts in his body and his mind. He hated it.

Coulson slipped out, and Arkady came after with the failures. Shane's body was cold, his teeth chattered, and his flesh felt numb, but he was glad to have them out.

"Is it done, then?" Arkady asked.

"Shaw and the Waste are destroyed. Hawke is dead. I think his whole team might be gone. I'd say we're done," Coulson replied.

"Very done." Shane looked at Ventura passed out on the floor. "Let's get the hell out of here."

# Epilogue

Coulson had to help Ventura make it back to one of Hawke's Humvees, which they used to escape the desert. Shane assured the agent that they were not stealing a U.S. military vehicle.

Arkady stayed behind with the failures underground. It was the only home they had known for many years, and Shane was just as happy to leave them in a place where it was unlikely anyone would see them again. They were too dangerous to be out in the world.

Shane drove past an unmanned security checkpoint on the way out of the desert and got on a road that led them back to Las Vegas. Ventura badly needed a hospital.

"That was something," Coulson said as the lights of the city appeared on the horizon ahead of them.

"That's one word for it," Shane agreed.

"I didn't poke around in there, for what it's worth," the ghost said.

"What?"

"In your head. I didn't look for anything. Wasn't the job, so... didn't look."

"Good," Shane said.

He would be lying if he'd said that he hadn't been worried about it. Even in his own head, he had a hard time convincing himself that it wasn't a concern. It wasn't just Coulson; it was the idea of anyone having access to his mind like that.

Despite everything they had been through together, Shane had reservations about the ghost. He'd had them since they met. Circumstances had altered his perception some, and he trusted Colson now. But, in the back of his mind, he held onto the fear of what would happen one day if he had to destroy Coulson. If he could even pull it off. Knowing that the ghost might now know that Shane thought that was not comforting.

Shane pulled the Humvee off in front of the emergency entrance at the hospital. They got Ventura into a wheelchair, and then Coulson left him. Ventura was unconscious immediately. His body had been run ragged, and the wounds on his back looked wet and angry.

"What happened to him?" a doctor asked when Ventura was wheeled in past the triage nurse's station.

"Burned by something out in the desert and was trapped out there for about a day," Shane said. "Not sure of all the details."

They transferred him to a gurney. The doctor stared at the wounds and grimaced, calling for help as someone cut away Ventura's clothes with scissors. They wheeled away the agent for treatment. Shane returned to the Humvee.

Shane knew the vehicle would easily be tracked. It had to be ditched. He drove it across the city and left it in an empty park before walking several blocks back in the direction he had come with Coulson at his side.

The ghost led them to the Golden Gate Towers, the hotel where Shane had first stayed when he arrived in Las Vegas. Someone had tried to kill him there, but that problem was solved.

The gambling ghosts were still in the parking lot. Only one bothered to look up as Shane walked up to the lot. The old, tired-looking ghost waved, and Shane nodded back.

One car was in the lot, parked under the only functional light. A woman leaned against the trunk drinking a large Starbucks coffee. Her hair was pulled back from her face into a loose ponytail. Shane recognized her immediately and almost asked how she knew to be there. Of course, that was a silly question.

"Look at you two sorry sights." Jillian set her drink on the trunk.

Coulson approached her with a smile. She spread her arms to offer him a hug, and he pulled back, offering a shrug instead.

"Not in the best shape, love," he told her.

She raised an eyebrow and reached out to touch his shoulder. Her hand passed through. Shane could see the cold feel of the ghost shock her, her pupils expanding and the hairs on her bare arm standing up before she pulled away.

"Should I be concerned?" she asked.

"It's getting better," Coulson told her. "Consider it like a post-biologic flu."

"Post-biologic. Classy," Jillian said.

She looked at Shane then, giving him a quick once-over.

"Looking rough, Mr. Ryan," she said.

"Feeling rough," he replied.

"Dezzy got a hold of me. I took a last-minute flight in; got here about an hour ago," she said. "He told me the world was ending and asked if I knew where Vincent was."

"Sounds about right," Coulson told her.

"He's still hunting for Vincent, but I take it the apocalypse was put on standby?"

"For the time being," Coulson said. "Took some work, though."

Jillian had already booked a room for Shane. They headed inside, and Shane chuckled. A pack of Lucky Strikes sat on the nightstand.

"You thought of everything," he said.

"That's my job," she reminded him. Her ability to read minds made it very easy to know what people wanted, where they were staying, and probably a lot more.

Coulson turned on the television, and Shane was about to tell him to leave it off when he realized what was on the screen. A reporter stood over a widespread pile of rubble. There were collapsed buildings and cars half-swallowed in a pile of dirt. It looked like a sinkhole had opened under a small town in the desert. On the screen were the words "Benton, Nevada".

The news detailed how the town had fallen into the earth after a gas leak caused an underground explosion, and so far, no bodies had been recovered. Of course, it was not what happened, but that was the story being shared.

A man from some government agency explained how dangerous it would be to exhume the remains of any townspeople, how the pocket had caused an instability, and how digging out the dead might kill even more people. They would fill in the hole and make it a memorial. None of the bodies would be removed.

There was no mention of Hawke on the news, of course. Nor the military, the desert labs, the Burnt Souls, Burners, the Waste, or Shane and Ventura. Nothing had happened except a gas leak that destroyed a little town in the middle of nowhere. The story quickly changed to one about an upcoming county fair.

"We should head out and find Dezzy before he assembles a superhero team to prevent the end of days," Jillian said.

"Yeah," Coulson agreed. He stood facing Shane with the half-cocky smile he always seemed to have on his face. "It's been weird, Ryan."

"It has," Shane agreed.

He held out his hand, and Coulson smiled properly, taking it in his. Even without his illusory physical form, they could shake.

"Don't be a stranger," Jillian said on the way out the door.

Shane grunted, and she laughed. Coulson followed her into the hallway. Shane went to the window and opened it then, pulling the room's lone, uncomfortable chair toward it and sitting. He lit one of the cigarettes and blew the smoke out the window as he watched Jillian and Coulson drive away.

✳ ✳ ✳

The next morning, Ventura was awake, bandaged, and looking like he'd spent the entire past week lost in the desert. His eyes were sunken, and his flesh was pale. Shane was told that the wound on Ventura's back was just starting a serious infection. He'd need skin grafts to treat the burn as it was a third-degree wound from shoulder to shoulder. They had him on antibiotics and expected he'd make a reasonable recovery.

"You lived," Shane said.

"I know. I need a raise," the agent replied.

"That mean you still have a job?"

"Had a call earlier. I'm needed back east when I've recovered. Someone credited me with discovering the accident in Benton."

"Had to be Jillian," Shane said. "Gas leak swallowed the town. Too dangerous to look for bodies."

"That's Coulson's friend? How did she…" Ventura said. "Nevermind. I think Coulson came by before he left town last night. Can't remember."

"Reasonable. You look like hell, Ventura."

"You're only saying that because I feel like hell."

"Maybe," Shane grinned.

He stood, and Ventura sighed, closing his eyes.

"You heading out?"

"Yeah. Long drive," he said.

"It is." Ventura nodded. "I need some sleep, anyway. I was scorched by nuclear ghost fire, you know. Were you ever scorched by nuclear ghost fire?"

"Can't say that I was," Shane said.

"Point for Xander Ventura," the other man said. "I'll see you around, Shane. You should get some rest, too. World's going to kill you one of these days; might as well take a minute while you can."

"I'll keep that in mind. Get well, Ventura."

He was asleep before Shane even left the room.

The drive back to Nashua was a long, slow one. It dragged on, but

Shane didn't mind. It was good to be nowhere, doing nothing. He knew that feeling wouldn't last forever.

Check out these best-selling series from our talented authors:

## GHOST STORIES

### RON RIPLEY

BERKLEY STREET SERIES
MOVING IN SERIES
HAUNTED COLLECTION SERIES
DEATH HUNTER SERIES

### IAN FORTEY

JIGSAW OF SOULS SERIES
CULT OF THE ENDLESS NIGHT SERIES

## SUPERNATURAL SUSPENSE

### A. I. NASSER

SLAUGHTER SERIES
SIN SERIES

### DAVID LONGHORN

NIGHTMARE SERIES
ASYLUM SERIES

### SARA CLANCY

THE BELL WITCH SERIES
BANSHEE SERIES

For a complete list of our new releases and best-selling horror books, visit
ScareStreet.com or scan the QR code below!

www.ingramcontent.com/pod-product-compliance
Lightning Source LLC
Chambersburg PA
CBHW050345030726
47503CB00008B/2618